Praise for Lauraine Snelling

"Two delightful holiday tales reflect the
true meaning of the Christmas season."
—*RT Book Reviews* on *Once Upon a Christmas*

"Snelling exceeds expectations
in this sensitively written account of
three women whose lives are forever altered by
the eruption of Mount St. Helens in 1980.... The
emotional takeaway of this novel is reminiscent
of Karen Kingsbury at her best. The characters'
issues are neither surface nor easily solved.
A challenging, fulfilling read."
—*RT Book Reviews* on *The Way of Women*

Praise for Jillian Hart

"A sweet book with lovable characters that
have problems to overcome with the help of
faith and the power of true love."
—*RT Book Reviews* on *Homespun Bride*

"Jillian Hart conveys heart-tugging emotional
struggles and the joy of remaining open
to the Lord's leading."
—*RT Book Reviews* on *Sweet Blessings*

"These sweet and gentle romances offer the
same rich detail and charming characters
readers have come to love in her other works."
—*The Romance Reader's Connection*
on *Heaven Knows*

LAURAINE SNELLING

has been writing books since 1980, both fiction and nonfiction, historical and contemporary, for adults and young readers. Lauraine's books consistently appear on CBA bestseller lists and are frequently featured in the Crossings Book Club. Lauraine and her husband, Wayne, live in California and have two grown sons.

JILLIAN HART

grew up on her family's homestead, where she helped raise cattle, rode horses and scribbled stories in her spare time. After earning her English degree from Whitman College, she worked in travel and advertising before selling her first novel. When Jillian isn't working on her next story, she can be found puttering in her rose garden, curled up with a good book or spending quiet evenings at home with her family.

Yuletide Treasure

Lauraine Snelling

Jillian Hart

HARLEQUIN® LOVE INSPIRED®

Recycling programs for this product may not exist in your area.

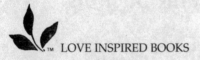

LOVE INSPIRED BOOKS

ISBN-13: 978-0-373-78799-9

YULETIDE TREASURE

Copyright © 2008 by Harlequin Books S.A.

The publisher acknowledges the copyright holder of the individual works as follows:

THE FINEST GIFT
Copyright © 2008 by Lauraine Snelling

A BLESSED SEASON
Copyright © 2008 by Jill Strickler

www.Harlequin.com

Printed in U.S.A.

CONTENTS

The Finest Gift

Lauraine Snelling

Chapter One

❧

Arley
Early December, 1910

Arlayna Louise Rachel Sharonn McGee Dexter, Arley
to everyone who knew her—her insistence that she be
called that was the one time she'd really stood up to her
grandmother—stared at the boxes of nutcrackers
stacked third shelf to the ceiling in the closet. Her great-
grandmother had begun the collection and the family
continued it to this day.

If she didn't start now, Christmas decorating would
be late. And the nutcrackers were always put out first.
She counted. Ten on the bottom shelf. As she pulled
them down she carefully removed each carved distinc-
tive soldier from its box and set it on the dining room
table. She moved to the next shelf and did the same, and
then the next, until she was reaching as high as she

could. At last she pulled over a needlepointed footstool, intending to stand on it.

"Oh, miss, let me go get the proper stool." Henny, the assistant housekeeper, stood behind her, wringing her hands, something she was often wont to do, around Arley at least.

"I'll be fine." Arley stepped onto the stool. "Oh, no!" As she grabbed for the shelf, one of the boxes went spinning over her shoulder.

Then, as if in slow motion, her fingers slipped off the shelf edge and she tumbled backward to land on top of the box, crushing it. The pain of her fall nearly made her cry out words her grandmother had washed out of her mouth years earlier. *"Uff da!"* had to suffice.

"Are you all right, miss?" Henny fluttered around Arley, living up to her namesake with little peeps of worry and flapping hands.

Arley sat up and craned her neck to see how badly the box was smashed. "There's no blood, so calm down." She crossed her legs Indian fashion and stood upright, the way one of her male cohorts had taught her years ago, back before her grandmother insisted she don the accoutrements of womanhood and cease running through the woods in childish games. "The *nutcracker* is what I'm concerned about." She flinched as she bent over to pick up the box. She'd have bruises for sure. Opening the box, she closed her eyes for a moment. Wouldn't you know this nutcracker happened to be her grandmother's favorite in the entire collection? Each year she told Arley the stories of the origins of each of the treasures. Except for this one. She always managed to divert the conversation when Arley asked about it. But it was always stationed in the center of the display.

"It's broken." She stared into Henny's horrified eyes. *Now what do I do?*

"Do you think it can be fixed?"

I most certainly hope so. Arley lifted the carved wooden nutcracker soldier from the box—in three pieces. "I don't know."

"There's the wood-carver who lives on the north side of Willow Creek. I've heard he can repair anything made of wood." Henny stared at the lower jaw, which was no longer connected to the face, then at Arley's eyes. "Do you want me take it there for you?"

"No, I caused the problem, so I'll have to fix it." Maxims like that had been drilled into Arley's brain ever since she'd come to live with her paternal grandmother twenty years ago. Her parents had been killed in a train wreck on the way home from Minneapolis, and the accident had taken more than her family; Arley had lost love and laughter. Her grandmother Louise believed children should be seen and not heard, and a young woman's life mission should be to take care of aging relatives. The huge house had seen more jollity in the years before her grandfather had died. But his grieving wife had never put away her widow's weeds.

Arley eyed the boxes of nutcrackers still on the shelves. While it was too early to put up the Christmas tree, the nutcrackers were always the first of the decorations to be put up and the last taken down. And here she'd been trying to be helpful.

She dusted off her hands and her posterior, which

fared better than she'd feared due to her padded wool petticoat and wool knickers under her wool serge skirt. Her grandmother disliked spending undue monies on coal for the furnace and wood for the fireplaces. But perhaps if she'd not been wearing fingerless wool gloves, she might not have lost her hold and fallen on the box.

"Grandmother will return soon and I want all the nutcrackers lined up on the dining room table and buffet. If we put them close together, surely she won't notice that one is missing."

"And if she asks?" Henny's pale eyebrows tickled her starched mobcap.

"I shall think of something." *Please, God, give me inspired thoughts before then.*

Soon, nutcrackers of all shapes and sizes filled both table and buffet, a colorful guard and testament to generations of gifts given first to her great-grandfather as a boy and handed down to Grandmother Louise. Being as there were no boys to inherit now, the collection would pass to Arley. The love of nutcrackers must be a male thing, she'd decided years earlier, as she would have much preferred angels and nativity scenes. Not that there weren't plenty of those, also. Decorating the mansion took an amazing amount of time and material. Her grandmother had put her in charge of the preparations when she turned fifteen, nearly ten years ago, as if conferring a title of great respect. Arley secretly thought her grandmother hoped such a job would help settle her down.

Arley forced herself not to limp as she made her way

to the kitchen, where a taller stool could be found in the butler's pantry. If only she'd fetched it, instead of standing on the needlepointed footstool. That was what being in a hurry did for one, and added one more errand to time that was already passing in a whirlwind.

"Will you be wanting lunch soon?" asked Mrs. Hanson, the cook.

"Grandmother will expect us to wait." Arley paused a moment to tuck strands of her mouse-brown hair back into the snood she usually wore to keep the curly mass under control. She thought of herself as exceedingly ordinary, not comely at all, as her grandmother so often reminded her. Yet she had a slightly turned-up nose and long eyelashes that framed sky-blue eyes. Her lithe figure would never need a corset, and she moved with a natural grace, inherited, along with her slender hands, from her mother.

"No, she sent word that she will be home later," Cook said.

"Oh." Then perhaps I can run to the wood-carver's house and be back before she returns. "Did she say why she was going to be late?"

"Something about the meeting taking longer than she had planned."

Arley knew her grandmother had a meeting with the lawyer and the banker who, under her careful supervision, managed her assets. While they thought they were her advisers, Louise Carlson Dexter kept up on all the business affairs and told them what to do, more often than not. She was known to be astute in all matters financial and did not suffer fools gladly. Since Arley was frequently called in to assist with her grand-mother's prodigious correspondence, she had a fairly good idea of the scope of her grandmother's business acumen and knowledge.

The fact that she'd not been asked to accompany her grandmother today had made her wonder what was in the offing. But instead of stewing about it, she'd set about getting the house decorations out and as much up as possible to forestall any hints of dalliance. Sometimes no matter how hard she tried to be ladylike, disaster followed like the smashed box and now an almost lie. "I'll have lunch later."

Ignoring Cook's questioning look, she tucked the badly bent box with the broken nutcracker into a cro-cheted bag and, dressing in her warmest cloak, long scarf, gloves, sapphire wool felt hat that tied in a bow under her chin, set out for the wood-carver's. Since her grandmother had the carriage, she resolved to take a shortcut through a copse of oak and maple trees that raised bent black arms and fingers to the vivid blue sky. When she kept sinking through the crust on the snow, she changed her mind and returned to follow the road that had been plowed by a team and scraper. Skis would have been the best mode of travel today, but she'd not worn the proper boots for the binding.

Plan ahead. Another of her grandmother's admonitions echoed in her mind. So true and proving her grandmother right again. But then, how could one plan for an accident?

On her way through the village, Arley paused at the window to the bookstore. The proprietress, who often invited her in for tea and a lively discussion on whatever book they were reading, waved from behind the display she was arranging for Christmas. When she held up a new book, Arley leaned closer to the glass to see the cover graced by two little blond girls and an enchanting Victorian dollhouse. She motioned to her friend, signaling she'd be right in. This would be a perfect book to read on the morrow at her weekly read-aloud to the children at the local orphanage. Charmed with her purchase, she continued on her errand. How she had dreamed of a dollhouse as a little girl, but that was another one of those dreams that ceased with the death of her parents. Her grandmother thought toys like that were frivolous.

Arley crossed the stone bridge that arched over rushing Willow Creek, the namesake of their little village in southern Minnesota. She saw a log house with a carved-wood sign suspended on a bracket above the door. Lawrence Gunderson, Woodworker. While the house seemed to invite her to come closer, she hesitated a moment, knowing that the wood-carver had a reputation as a recluse and curmudgeon. How had she lived in Willow Creek all these years without knowing more about him?

She took her courage in both hands, pretended she was her grandmother and strode to the door. Should she rap or go right on in? Since this was by signage a place of business, she pressed down on the levered door opener and entered a room, dim in contrast to the bright white snow outside. Blinking, she stamped the snow off her boots on the rug provided and shut the door behind her.

She stared around the room, which was heated by an arched stone fireplace on one wall and decorated with shelves of carved clocks, ornate boxes and beautifully turned bowls and platters behind a well-worn counter. A grandfather clock ticked away in one corner and a cuckoo popped out of a house on the wall to announce the hour. The grandfather clock answered in deep bongs that befit its size and station. She didn't see a nutcracker anywhere. Perhaps he'd refuse the repair, wherever he was. She hoped not.

She heard a muttering from behind a faded curtain that hung across a doorway in the back wall. "Hello?" When there was no answer, she raised her voice. "Hello, is anyone here?"

"Yes! What do you want?" The curtain flew to the side at the entrance of a Viking straight off the pages of a picture book. Tall, with shoulders so broad they nearly touched the doorjamb, hair that needed a trimming but glinted gold in the light, a wide brow and carved granite jaw, the Viking had a glare that preceded him.

"Are you Mr. Gunderson, the wood-carver?" She kept herself from taking a step backward by sheer force of will. Somehow she had thought of him as an older man and while the shoulders matched her impression, he was too young. Had this fellow taken over the old man's business?

"No!" The glare from under bushy eyebrows did not abate. He clamped his arms over a chest that pushed against the buttons of his linen shirt. It was the sort that was full in the sleeves, gathered into the shoulders and was worn by swashbuckling pirates. While her mind cataloged the information, his rudeness shocked her almost too much to respond. Almost but not quite.

"I beg your pardon." Each syllable snapped in air that had thickened between them. "I came to see Mr. Gunderson."

"He's not here."

Her jaw clamped shut and furrows deepened in her forehead. Whatever possessed him?

"Come back tomorrow!" He turned and headed back to the curtain.

"Of all the…" Ignoring her grandmother's oft-uttered but rarely used admonition that one always caught more bees with honey than vinegar, Arley took a step forward. "If your employer knew the way you treated a customer, I'm sure you would find yourself outside in a snowbank, sir. You are insufferable."

The curtain swished behind him.

The urge to follow him, to rip that faded blue cloth aside, made her take two more steps forward. But since at the moment she couldn't think of anything vile enough to say, she turned and wrenched the stubborn front door open, taking her ire and the broken toy with her. The door did not even slam, no matter that she'd tried to close it.

"Well, I never!" As the breeze caught her breath, she stomped down the path to the road and headed for the bridge. She'd crossed the bridge when the enormity of what she had done assailed her. What would her grandmother say if she heard that her granddaughter had castigated a shopkeeper? And surely in a village as small as Willow Creek, someone had heard her screeching.

Arlayna Louise Rachel Sharonn McGee Dexter, you'd better go back and apologize. Both manners and the good book would agree. Ignoring her internal orders, she strode on home.

Chapter Two

Nathan

Carving the fittings for a violin took an amazing amount of patience.

Nathan David Gunderson returned to his task, wondering if he could come up with a good reason for wanting to make his own violin. Yes, the piano that had shattered upon being dropped by the carters had provided him with excellent wood for his creation. Yes, he loved to play the violin. Yes, he loved learning woodworking at his grandfather's side. But why try to make a violin so early in his training? Was he a masochist of the first order? Not that this was his first project. All those years ago when, as a boy, he had come to visit his grandfather and learned to use the tools remained the only bright spot in a life dominated by a father who thought music a hobby not a career. Nathan was in line to inherit the Twin Cities Coal Company, and his father would see him prepared to step into his shoes. Or he would know the reason why.

Nathan studied the pieces he'd been working on. What had started out as a productive morning had disintegrated upon the arrival of that young woman. He refused to call her a lady after the way she lambasted him. But her apparel had not been that of a common person. The cut of her bonnet and the fine wool of her coat bespoke money. Who was she?

He drove the thought away by picking up a sandstone to bring the shine out in the wood. His hand shook slightly, a reminder of the horrific explosion that nearly took his life at the coal plant. The fragrance of cherry wood released by the sanding freed his mind from the unpleasant recollection.

A few minutes later the chirp of the cat that wound around his ankles drew his attention.

"You need to go out?"

She flicked her tail and padded for the back door.

Never having had pets of his own, Nathan had fallen prey to the imperious demands of Eugenia, as his grandfather called his fluffy gray housecat. A queen's name suited her. And since her kittens had been born in the box by the stove, she spent little time on his lap or the bench where his carved pieces were all laid out in perfect order. Until she became *enceinte,* she had supervised his work with unblinking green eyes.

He let the cat out and waited for her to do her business in the pile of sawdust they kept for that purpose. The day was glorious, the sun setting afire the snow-tipped branches of the trees beyond the garden that now lay hidden under a glistening white blanket. He glanced to the side of the doorway where his snowshoes stood propped against the wall. When carving grew too frustrating, he often trekked off through the woods until exhaustion drove him home again.

Eugenia shook her paws, each one separately, and padded back inside to sit on the rug in front of the fire and proceeded to groom away any trace of her outing, at the moment ignoring the mewlings of her progeny. Even though their eyes were yet to open, the four kittens could cry loud enough to wake Nathan from a sound sleep at night. Yet she could ignore them.

Nathan cut two slices of bread, enough cheese to cover and added beef already sliced, then slapped the two halves together and, chewing as he wandered, went to stand over the remains of the piano. There was plenty of wood there for other violins and still leave plenty of clock or box material for his grandfather.

Why had the woman become so incensed with him? After all, he'd come when she called, not waiting for her to ring the bell on the counter. Strange female, really. He strolled back to the workbench where he had the neck of the future violin clamped in two vises, with one-inch-thick boards the length of the neck on either side. He smoothed gentle fingers over the newly glued case that yet needed a top. The wood grain on the under piece matched that on the top, which still lay off to the side.

He heard the brush of boots against the scraper on the back stoop. His grandfather had returned. Shame he hadn't been there earlier to wait on the young woman.

"So how goes it?" Lawrence Gunderson unwrapped his scarf from around his neck and hung it with coat and hat on the pegs along the wall by the door.

"I hoped to have the top glued, also."

"So what stopped you?" Lawrence rubbed his silvered hair back with the palms of both hands. "Is the coffee hot?"

"No, sir, I forgot all about the coffee." Nathan looked toward the kitchen stove and realized that he'd not put any wood in it or—he glanced at the clock—too many hours for there to be any flame left. He had kept the fireplace stoked, however, or he would have noticed the cold. "Sorry." The rule was that whoever stayed to home was supposed to keep the fire burning and the coffeepot ready to pull forward to heat quickly.

"Ah, lad. Don't you know there is nothing more important than hot coffee after the walk from the station?" Lawrence rattled the grate before lifting the lid so see the lack of coals. "Did your mother teach you nothing?"

"Nothing that would be helpful here with you. And I'd just as soon forget most of what I learned." He suffered no inclination to return to city life, being content here with his grandfather in a backwater where most people didn't even know his name or that he was here, for that matter.

"Now, don't go getting your dander up." Lawrence glanced into the wood box. "We could use some wood in here."

Nathan flinched. That was another of his jobs, keeping the wood boxes filled. After one attempt at cooking, he'd been relegated to hauling wood and water. Life in a mansion in Minneapolis was a far cry from living in a humble wood-carver's cabin. The store, if you could call it that, took up the front room across the width of the building, and the workroom and kitchen were behind. There was one long bedroom upstairs, and Nathan could stand only in the middle of it, as the roof sloped steeply to the low walls.

"Bring in that haunch of venison before you start with the wood. I'll carve us off some steaks for supper." Lawrence had bought half a deer from a man in the village who enjoyed hunting. While he'd smoked the front quarter, the weather had been cold enough to hang and freeze the hind quarter. As long as it was hung too high for any marauding four-footed creature, they could hack at it until it was gone.

"Of course."

Later that evening after supper as they sat reading before the fire, Nathan remembered. "Grandfather, a young woman came by to see you today."

Lawrence looked up from his magazine. "Who?"

"I have no idea. I told her to come back tomorrow." He lowered his book. "You will be here tomorrow, correct?"

"I don't deliver clocks every day, you know."

Nathan knew that his grandfather didn't usually deliver his wares, expecting the customers to come and pick them up, but he'd taken two boxes with an assortment of his work into St. Paul to be displayed in a new store.

"Can you describe her?"

Nathan slowly shook his head. "Average, I suppose.

She wore a thick cloak and a blue bonnet with a brim that framed her face. Her eyes were framed by lashes so long they—" He stopped.

"Average, you say?" The older man raised an eyebrow.

Nathan ignored the teasing. "She carried a string bag, but I have no idea what was in it." She'd left in a snit. He thought back to their conversation, if one could call it that. As he replayed the scene in his mind, confusion dogged him again. He'd been working on the pegs for the violin, and when he heard a voice call, his knife slipped and he… He glanced down at his thumb where a thin red line showed how close he had come to a bad cut. *Brusque* might be the term to describe his attitude, though she'd called him *rude*. "I just told her you weren't in and to return tomorrow."

"You didn't offer to look at what she wanted done and suggest she leave it for me to work on?"

Nathan shook his head. "No. Though that would have been the polite thing." But all he'd wanted to do was get back to his work. He glanced up to see sadness settle on his grandfather like a flock of crows. "She seemed mightily opinionated."

"But no name."

"No." Because I didn't ask her. *Mea culpa*. His years of Latin came in handy at times, especially when castigating himself.

"Well, we can hope she *does* return. I'd hate to have a customer unhappy with me. This is too small a village to allow rancor to develop." The old man went back to his newspaper and Nathan rose to check on his last glue application. His book hadn't kept his attention, anyway. He glanced over his shoulder a few minutes later to see his grandfather with his head back on the chair, mouth open, eyes closed and Eugenia on his lap, a typical evening tableau.

He picked up his drawing tablet and, taking it and a pencil back to his chair and the lamp, worked again on the drawing of the violin neck. His book had mentioned a slight change in the carved scroll that would be very attractive. If he were to have his dream of producing violins for concert performers, he needed to develop some sort of unique attribute. He laid his drawing aside. How could he be so foolish as to dream of his violins in concerts when he hadn't even finished the first one? The tone was the thing, and that came from the violin itself. What set a Stradivarius so above the rest? If only he could take one apart and study each piece. Not that one would ever take apart a treasure like that, but how wonderful it would be to measure and inspect the instrument in minute detail.

He closed his eyes for a moment but instead of seeing his violin, the young woman wearing a sapphire-blue bonnet that shaded snapping eyes demanded his attention. No woman had appeared in his mind like this since before the accident, the cataclysmic event that sent his life spinning off in a new direction.

Chapter Three

Arley

Don't be a ninny. Just open the door.

How silly to be frightened of opening the door. The cabin was a place of business and the sign in the window said Open. But then, it had said that the day before, too. Arley kept talking to herself, but she continued to stand rooted to the stoop. Or frozen there, since it was indeed winter.

You must apologize. The voice sounded amazingly like that of her grandmother. In fact, had she not known better, she would have turned to make sure she'd not been followed. At least her grandmother hadn't realized that one of the nutcrackers was missing. *If you stand out here much longer, someone is sure to notice, and guess who they'll report to?* She never had gotten away with anything in her hoyden days. She'd sometimes thought her grandmother sent out spies who raced back to the mansion to report before she could get back herself.

Arley gave herself a shake and reached out to press down on the metal latch. With a firm push, the door swung inward. Nothing like gathering courage to brave the dragon, as the heroine so often did in the stories she'd devoured as a girl. She stepped over the threshold and paused for her eyes to adjust to the dimness. That was one thing about log cabins—they generally didn't have a lot of windows, although the show window off to her right had been nicely arranged.

Again, no one was in the front room. *Please, Lord, let the wood-carver be here today, not that arrogant bear of a man.* Her mind returned to delight in the timbre of his voice. The rich baritone would have sounded much better laughing, instead of being unpleasant. His identity had bedeviled her the past evening. This time she saw a bell on the counter and crossed to pick it up and ring it. The silver chime tinkled brightly in the still air.

She heard a *thunk* behind the curtain and a voice.

"Coming."

This was definitely not the voice from the day before. How could one word sound so welcoming?

A barrel-chested man, with a smile that turned up his mustache and a bald pate rising through a circle of fluffy silver, pushed through the curtain. "Good morning. A fine day, is it not?"

She nodded and smiled back at him. "Yes, it is indeed." She held out her string bag. "I came yesterday to ask for your help."

"And my grandson told you I'd be in today."

"That's right." *He shouted it at me, to be precise, but we won't go into that.*

"I am Lawrence Gunderson, proprietor and woodcarver." He extended his hand and smiled again. When she just nodded, he leaned forward slightly. "And you are?"

"Oh, pardon me. I am Miss Dexter. I'm sure you know my grandmother."

"Ah, yes. Mrs. Arthur Dexter. I knew her when she was Louise Carlson, more than a few years ago. *Now* I know where I've seen you. Trailing behind her, carrying her baskets and fetching when she orders. Age has not been gentle with Louise."

Arley stared at him. The young man shouted and the old man made remarks too pointed for such a casual acquaintanceship. "You knew, er, know my grandmother?"

"In a village the size of ours, it would be difficult to grow up without knowing most of the inhabitants."

"Then how come you didn't know me?" *Arlayna Louise Rachel Sharonn McGee Dexter, what on earth is the matter with you? Letting your mouth get away with itself like that!* Again the voice of her grandmother with a little huff of her own thrown in.

"I was living in the west for many years and only returned two years ago. It is easier to stay in the background, don't you think?" His eyes twinkled, but his brows arched in a knowing look. "Besides, you've changed a great deal since I left."

"I see." Arley straightened her shoulders and pulled in her chin. "Well, I have a problem I am hoping you might be able to solve. I was taking out all the nutcrackers to decorate the house with and I—" she drew the box from her bag and held the sorry spectacle out "—fell on this one."

"Oh, my goodness, I hope you didn't hurt yourself." He looked at her as if assessing damage, taking the box in hand at the same moment.

"More my pride than anything else, but the nutcracker suffered the most." She watched him remove the top of the box and stare down into the interior. "Please, I do hope you can fix it. This is my grandmother's favorite. If she knew of the damage, she would be most upset." Arley felt as if she was running in place, her words going faster and faster. She stared at him as he stared into the box.

"Is…is it that bad?" Her voice trembled. Not that she was afraid of her grandmother's rage, but she would hate to see her upset. This was the woman who had taken her in and given her a home all these years. She might want to scream and stamp her feet in frustration sometimes, but she loved the old woman dearly.

When he finally raised his head, she caught a look in his eye, that had he not blinked it away, made her think of tears. One tear or a pool. Surely she'd been wrong.

"Ah, I am sorry, Miss Dexter. Just an old man's forgetfulness. But of course I can repair the nutcracker. I hope you do not need it by tomorrow, for it will take a bit of time. But when I am finished, your grandmother will never know this gentleman had an accident."

Arley forcibly kept herself from grabbing the

counter to keep standing, so weak at the knees did she feel. "Oh, I cannot thank you enough. For a few moments there I feared the worst." She heard noises from the other room that sounded like something crying. When she cocked her head to listen, the old man chuckled.

"Eugenia just returned to her kittens. They quite resent it when she leaves them and like to tell her so."

"Kittens? You have kittens?"

"Four of them, all of whom will be looking for homes before Christmas. Their eyes are just opening. Would you like to see them?"

"May I? I mean, the mother won't mind?" Kittens. All her life she'd wanted a dog or a cat, but her grandmother wouldn't allow animals in the house. At least she could look at them and dream.

"This way." With the nutcracker and box in one hand, he held the faded blue curtain aside with the other, beckoning her to precede him. She stepped from the display room into a much larger room that appeared to be divided in two by some invisible line. On one side were clocks and boxes, small tables and simple chairs all in various states of completion. A workbench with shelves above and below, along with tools lined up on pegs between bench and upper shelves, took up one entire wall. On the other wall a fire crackled in a stone fireplace faced by two worn but comfortable-looking easy chairs. An oval braided rug sat between chairs and fire. A kitchen with cast-iron stove, counters and shelves and a table and chairs took up another quarter of the space, with the drop-leaf table in front of a window overlooking the woods behind the house.

All this she saw in an instant, then her gaze focused on the man working at the bench on what looked to be a violin. The fragrance of wood shavings permeated the air, not unlike the scent of cedar that filled the mansion now that she had cedar and pine garlands wrapping the banisters.

"Miss Dexter, I'd like you to meet my grandson, Nathan Gunderson. Nathan, Miss Dexter."

The Viking laid down his tools and turned to greet her. He ducked his head just a bit as if out of some sense of courtesy. "Miss Dexter."

Arley felt her temper sizzle a little. The nerve of him. Two could play this game. "Mr. Gunderson." At least he wasn't growling at her the way he was yesterday.

"Miss Dexter has brought me a nutcracker to repair, and I'm showing her the kittens."

"I see."

The younger Mr. Gunderson could take lessons in manners from his grandfather. *Apologize! No, I don't think so! Arlayna Louise... Don't start with that,* she ordered the voice in her head. *I am going to look at the kittens, go read to my children and go home. I will return for the nutcracker and then I won't be seeing either of them again. So I do not need to apologize.* All the while her mind was throwing fiery darts back and forth, she followed the older man to a wooden box lying off to one side of the stove. A fluffy gray cat lay on her side with four kittens busily nursing. She blinked up at her visitors and went back to cleaning a front paw. One kitten was mostly white, another all gray, at least from what she could see of them. Another gray one had white front paws with which he was kneading his mother's belly. The last one had a hint of tiger stripes in the gray.

"They are so precious!" She smiled at her host. "I've never seen kittens so tiny." She thought of dropping to her knees and stroking first the beautiful mother and then each of the squirming babies. The thought of having one of her own was like a pain in her heart.

"When they are old enough, you may have the pick of the litter, you know." His voice went up on the last syllable, in the charming way of those of Scandinavian heritage.

Was he Norwegian like her grandmother? Surely they had known each other; they looked to be about the same age. And yet, she'd never heard his name mentioned. But then, if he'd been gone for a long time, perhaps Grandmother Louise had just forgotten. Not that the woman had forgotten anything in all the years Arley had known her. "That's not possible." With a sigh, Arley straightened. "I must be going. Thank you for agreeing to fix the nutcracker."

"Wouldn't you stay for some coffee? It can be ready in a few minutes."

"Thank you, but no. I have a date with some children who are waiting to hear the next chapter in the book I'm reading to them."

"You are a schoolteacher?"

"No. I read at the orphanage every week and they are expecting me. When should I return for the nutcracker?"

"I will let you know." He led her back to the curtain.

She caught the look of puzzlement he cast at the younger man, who was now sanding a piece of wood as if his life depended on it being just right. "Goodbye, Mr. Gunderson." She raised her voice the slightest and smiled inwardly when he started and looked up at her.

"G-good day."

"Thank you again." She stepped over the threshold when Lawrence held the door open for her. "I'll look forward to picking up the nutcracker. Goodbye."

"Enjoy your reading." He closed the door behind her and she lifted her face to the sun's rays. Now to decide on a present for her grandmother. The thought of the broken nutcracker had taken up her mind. Or was it the Viking, Odin of the carving tools, who preoccupied her? *Don't be silly,* she chided herself as she strode off to the orphanage, past the courthouse and the Carnegie Library that provided her with such constant pleasure in books and a place where she could be helpful and out of her grandmother's sight. Then she passed the bookstore where she'd purchased the book about the dollhouse. She'd read the first chapters of the story last night and knew her children would love to hear it. Her father had promised her they'd make a dollhouse one day. What would her life have been like had her parents not died? She'd mentioned her dream of having a dollhouse to her grandmother only once. She'd been good even then at burying her feelings when they got stomped on.

Chapter Four

Nathan

"Interesting."

Nathan turned to look at his grandfather. While he'd tried to ignore the silence since the young woman left, he'd sneaked peeks over his shoulder to see his grandfather studying the broken toy. "What is?"

"Not what, but who." He fitted two pieces of the wooden figure together and held them up.

Nathan waited and when it seemed nothing more was forthcoming, returned to his work on the violin. "I assume you are referring to the young woman." To whom he should have been far more polite yesterday. Guilt nagged like an aching tooth. Where had he left his manners? What was there about her that brought out such a contentious reaction in him? After all, he'd been turning away females all his life, most of them more interested in the family fortune than who he was. He knew he was good-looking—any glance in the mirror told him that—but since the accident his face had become more rugged, as if a wood-carver had chiseled away any surplus skin and flesh to reveal harsh bones and thundering eyebrows. What used to be laugh lines had been dug down to slashes, some of them carved by pain and possibly something he was not ready to admit, even to a mirror. Explosions were life changing if one was fortunate enough to live through the event.

He unclenched his hand from the sanding block and after inhaling a deep breath and letting it all out, stretched his fingers, clenched them again and repeated the action. The doctor had warned him about remaining in any one position too long. He needed to keep moving and stretching so that he didn't end up crippled. Not that he wasn't already, if only on the inside.

"Aching again?" His grandfather's voice came softly from down the workbench.

"Not enough to worry about." Nathan held the piece he was working on up to the light and stroked his finger over and around the smooth surface. Smooth yes, but not yet finished quality. Something like much of his burned and healed skin, mostly hidden by long-sleeved shirts buttoned nearly to the collar and long underwear that helped hold the Minnesota winter cold at bay. The back of his left hand wore the only visible scar.

The way he'd treated that young woman was evidence of the internal ones.

The smell of wood glue permeated the room. Between that and the scent of the cherry wood he was sanding, the place smelled of home and comfort and love. Scents to be found only here and never in St. Paul—at his father's house.

He glanced over to see his grandfather placing one part of the broken toy into a vise and painting the broken edges with the glue. "You can fix it?"

"Of course. Louise will never know of the accident when I am finished."

"You know her grandmother, then?"

"Yes. We were good friends—at one time."

Had Nathan not been paying close attention, he might have missed the final words. Was there a story here he'd never heard? Not that he'd have heard any of the family stories, if his father had his way. When he left his father's home near Fargo, he'd resolved never to look back. Said there was nothing there to bring him back. Nothing, including his own father, his mother having died years earlier. That he'd allowed his son visits to Willow Creek in the summer was due to providence, something his grandfather referred to as God's intervention, giving them both a gift.

Nathan watched the old man daubing glue most precisely and decided to pursue the topic. "What happened?"

"Life got in the way, I s'pect." Lawrence fitted the opposing piece into the wood, matching up each jagged piece like a surgeon putting a bone back together. Then after studying it, he tightened the clamp, checked it again and nodded. "How about a cup of coffee? Mrs. Mueller sent us a portion of her prize stollen."

Nathan crossed to the stove and inserted several chunks of wood into the firebox, then set the stove lids back in place. He pulled the coffeepot forward, lifted the lid and checked the contents. At home, Cook would have thrown out the remainder and started over, but his grandfather refused to be so profligate with his stores, even reusing coffee grounds. He abhorred waste of any kind, from coffee grounds to people who overlooked important things like love and family. Nathan fetched the stollen from the intricately carved bread box, and after cutting off several slices, set them on a plate and put the plate in the oven. Ah, the lessons he'd learned since coming here to Willow Creek. Learning to live without servants had not been the ordeal his father had predicted.

As they finished their coffee, Lawrence turned to his grandson. "I think it time you begin to work with the lathe. I have some nice pieces of wood for bowls once you get good enough."

Nathan nodded. While he'd rather work on his violin, he had agreed to learn all the skills his grandfather could teach him. Turning wood with the lathe was a good next step.

"When I was in the cities, I looked at an engine that would turn it for us, but for the moment you must learn the old way. I remember I had more trouble getting the rhythm of the treadle than I did with the actual piece. I have some branches out back that will do for starters. We'll need to spend some time tonight sharpening gouges."

Nathan nodded. Gouges carved the pattern in turned wood. They never had enough turned spindles for all the tables and chairs they made. Why, one could spend all day at the lathe. He probably should have volunteered to start on that some time ago. He rinsed out their coffee cups and turned them upside down on the counter. The stollen had hit the spot. He had a feeling Mrs. Mueller would like to provide more than occasional baked goods, but his grandfather always kindly rebuffed her.

The hours his mother had made him spend in dance class put him in good stead as he rhythmically pumped the treadle to start the wood spinning. Holding the gouge steady was another matter.

"You take off all the bark first with this one." Lawrence handed him a flat inch-wide gouge. "Just hold the sharp end against the wood and move slowly to your right. Sort of like peeling an apple."

Working the foot pedal and keeping the shavings flowing evenly were two different things. At a knot in the wood, the gouge jumped out of his hands and went spinning across the counter.

"You have to look ahead to see what is coming."

"Talk about a metaphor for life," Nathan grumbled to himself the third time he had to fetch the gouge. But finally he had the bark off and a fairly clean planing surface. He took his foot off the treadle and stepped back. "What do you want of this?"

"Let's make legs for a hassock." The old man dug in a drawer and pulled out a well-worn pattern. "This is easy for a starter. The piece is long enough to make two legs at a time. Start with the half-inch gouge. You need to mark the center with a pencil."

Nathan did exactly as he was told, but several hours

later, his finished pieces bore only a faint resemblance to other similar pieces.

"You did well."

"No, I did not do even tolerably. Those two legs will never appear on a hassock or anything else." He shook his head. "Although they will make good firewood." He glanced down at the pile of wood curls at his feet. "You ever thought of bagging this stuff up and selling it as fire starter?"

His grandfather rolled his eyes at the suggestion and took his place at the lathe. "Just watch." Within minutes the grooves were smoothed out and the ridges sharpened up. The pieces would need far less sanding to attain the finish needed. "It just takes practice."

Nathan clamped in another piece. No sense getting out the saw until he had several to cut apart. He shrugged to work out the tightness in his shoulders and set his foot to the treadle. Good thing he didn't need a lathe to craft his violin.

The next piece of wood shattered and sent slivers in every direction, including his chin. He leaped back, muttering some words he'd perfected in the hours of dealing with pain from the burns. One piece had flown clear over by the fireplace; others were scattered on the bench and floor.

"Here, you better let me bandage your chin," Lawrence suggested.

"Why?" Nathan swiped at his chin and stared at his hand. "I'm bleeding!"

"That's why I suggest the bandage. This kind of thing happens sometimes. I should have warned you."

"I thought it was pine wood, not dynamite." Nathan sat down in the chair his grandfather indicated and pressed his fingers against the wound to stop the bleeding.

Lawrence fetched the medicine kit and after cleaning the gash, applied cotton folded into a square and taped it in place. "There, that ought to hold it." He pulled some splinters out of his grandson's hair and brushed them off his arms and shoulders. "Good thing you have a long-sleeved shirt on."

"Is there any way to tell from looking at a piece of wood how much it will splinter?"

"Not to my knowledge. But this one was a mite dramatic. Wood is somewhat like people, you know. You can't always tell by looking on the outside what's in their hearts."

Nathan hung his head and ran his fingers through his hair, releasing more wood bits. That piece of wood was just like his life, shattered under pressure. Not that he'd been happy starting at the bottom and working up into being head of the company but he'd been doing it, following the training path his father had laid out for him. But after the fire, he hadn't shattered just in body, but in mind, too. Soon his father would insist he return to his position.

But he couldn't go back. No, he *wouldn't* go back. His father had men who would love to run the Twin Cities Coal Company. They just weren't his son. His only son. Besides, his father had plenty of years left in him yet to keep the company growing and making more money for both him and the investors. While he,

Nathan, stayed here and convinced these pieces of wood that they would like to become part of something either beautiful or necessary or some blend of the two.

He heaved himself to his feet. Another hour, another turned spindle, leg or whatever. He would learn this.

The pile of shavings had grown huge before he stopped for the day. He took his turned pieces of wood to the window. Outside, the setting sun was sending ribbons of light that flickered off the snow-laden branches of the hardwood forest behind the house. He inspected the pieces of wood, eyeing them for matches in size and patterns, and looking for faults.

His grandfather stopped planing a walnut board and joined him at the table, watching as Nathan divided the work into three piles. "You've come a long way for your first day."

Nathan gestured at the piles in turn. "These are keepers, these need more work and these will help keep us warm tonight."

Lawrence chuckled. "We have firewood aplenty." He picked up one piece that was thicker than the others. "This could become a pair of good candleholders—the fatter, more decorative kind."

"Who uses candles any longer? In the city there is electricity now, as well as gaslights. Candles are passé."

"There is nothing cheerier than candlelight. Let me finish them and you will see." Lawrence studied each of the others. "A few days of this and you'll be ready to work on oak and maple. You'll find each wood a bit different to work with."

"I think I like fitting pieces together, like the clocks

and my violin. You know I dream of creating violins that will rival Stradivarius."

"I know, but sometimes one has to learn skills to keep a roof over one's head and food in the belly in order to live long enough to make a dream come true. It's like all the years you've been learning the coal business, to make your father happy and have a livelihood."

As if there was any chance this dream of his could come true.

"Why don't you play for me while I make the supper?"

"I think it is my turn to cook."

"As I said, why don't you play for me?" His grandfather's eyes twinkled.

"Are you saying my cooking is not much better than my work at the lathe?"

"Do not try to put words in my mouth." Lawrence pointed at the violin case resting safe on its shelf. "I do like to hear you play. It comforts me, and fills my heart with contentment."

Nathan blinked. Never had anyone said such things about his violin playing. He knew he was good at it and he knew it did those same things for him, but he also knew he could not be the concert player he had dreamed of being years ago. Then, he'd had to take his place in his father's empire. And as his father had said more than once, "Put away childish things." Even his father could quote scripture when the need was there.

As always, playing calmed him, and he went to bed

floating on the peace his grandfather said he felt, too. Until visions of a young woman kneeling in awe at the kitten nursery left him lying awake.

Chapter Five

Arley

"You think we could ever have a house like that, miss?"

Arley gazed down at four-year-old Nettie, who was still stroking the book Arley had been reading and now had lying in her lap. Arley started to say something, but one of the other girls gave Nettie a push.

"Don't be a ninny. Orphans don't get no dollhouses like that."

"Orphans don't get dolls."

"I had a doll once."

"Ah, you're lyin'."

"I did. My ma made it for me afore she died."

Arley leaned forward and spoke softly into the circle of girls ranging from the two-year-old sitting on an older girl's lap to the ten-year-old who should have been down in the kitchen helping prepare dinner but had wheedled her way into coming to story hour. "Now girls, let's not argue. After all, Christmas is coming and who knows what Saint Nicholas will bring?"

The girls all stared at her, mouths hanging open, as if she were speaking a foreign language. The older ones started shaking their heads and, one by one, rose and left the group. The little ones stared after them, then turned back to Arley and gave her sad smiles. When Nettie was the last one still leaning against her knees, Arley stroked her head. What could she say? Sure they all attended church and she and other townspeople brought gifts at Christmas. They made sure everyone had a good dinner, but they all went home to presents under the tree, more food than anyone could eat and games and singing. Families had memories to share, along with the cookies and candies.

If only her grandmother would let her bring some of these children home with her, at least to visit, to have a hot bath and perhaps a new dress. But the old woman was adamant. They would do what they could for the poor, but not in her own house.

Arley lifted Nettie onto her lap and stroked the wispy near-white hair back from a broad brow. "I'm glad you like the story."

"Oh, I do. Will you come again to read to us?"

"Yes, next week."

"So far away?" Nettie stroked the lace on one of Arley's cuffs. "So pretty."

"Thank you." Next week Arley planned to come with hair ribbons for all of them, something pretty of their own to have. She picked up her book and the two of them stared at the dollhouse on the cover. What if? Her mind leaped into the game. What if she brought the children a dollhouse? Where could she get one this late in the season? What if she made it? Who would help her? Would her grandmother like to help? She shook her head at that. This wasn't a useful gift, the kind her grandmother always insisted upon. But what if she gave the dollhouse to the girls at the orphanage in her grandmother's name, as a gift from her? The whole thing would be her own gift to her grandmother. Would it evoke her grandmother's displeasure again? Arley bit her lip, thinking. Even if Grandmother was unhappy with Arley's decision, at least the orphanage would have a dollhouse. She could also commission another nutcracker from Mr. Gunderson to add to the collection. Could he get one done in time?

And the most important question of all, would the wood-carver help her make the dollhouse? Did she dare ask? This was too exciting an idea to keep to herself, and she couldn't tell her grandmother. But if he was willing to help her, what about the Viking? She could just see his look of contempt for a prosaic dollhouse that would take time away from his work on his violin.

At the ringing of a bell for preparing for supper, Nettie slipped to the floor, dropped a kiss on Arley's hand and scampered off.

"Thank you for coming," Mrs. Teigen, the head of the orphanage, said as Arley drew her cloak around her shoulders and prepared for the frigid walk home. Had she realized it was so cold she would have allowed

Hanson, her grandmother's all-around man, to bring the sleigh when he'd offered.

"You are welcome. I so enjoy my time with them." Arley refrained from mentioning the dollhouse until she was sure it would happen. Surely she didn't need permission to bring a special gift at Christmas. "See you next week?"

Mrs. Teigen glanced outside. "Of course. Are you sure we shouldn't call your driver for you? It's snowing."

"No, I love to walk in the snow." Arley tucked her scarf in around her neck and her book into her pocket. With her hands snug in her mittens, she stepped out the door and paused at the top of the steps to soak up the beauty around her—big fat flakes of snow drifting down, covering the old dingy snow with new white fluff. The clouds seemed close enough to touch, blotting out the sun, bringing a dusky light in the middle of the afternoon.

Arley struck off for home, running a few steps and sliding when she was sure no one was watching. But the more she thought of the dollhouse, the faster she walked. If it weren't late, she'd have gone by the wood-carver's shop right then and asked for his assistance. How could she bear to wait until tomorrow?

"You shoulda called me, Miss Arley," Hanson said when he met her at the door. "I was about to get the sleigh out." He fussed as he took her cloak, shook off the snow and hung it on the hall tree until it could dry off.

"Ah, Hanson, can't you see how beautiful it is out?"

"Cold enough to freeze your nose. What would your grandmother say if I let something happen to you?"

"She'd say it was my fault, after she scolded me for being careless. But there is something magical about walking in the falling snow. And besides, it makes me feel more like Christmas."

"*Ja,* yes, of course. As if you needed to feel more like Christmas." He nodded at all the garlands, pinecones, red plaid bows and candles.

"The house does look lovely, doesn't it?"

He stepped closer and lowered his voice. "Did you get the…the gentleman repaired?"

Arley nodded and whispered back, "He's in the repair shop and I'll check on it tomorrow. Promised to be as good as new."

"Herself has been studying the collection."

"Maybe I should move them around again so she doesn't—"

"I think that'd be a very good idea." He stepped back and resumed normal speech. "Your grandmother is in the library. I have a fire going in there and Mrs. Hanson is to bring tea as soon as you arrive. I'll go tell her."

"Thank you, Hanson." She lowered her voice again. "I have something exciting to discuss with you. I'll need your help to keep it a secret."

"Oh, land, you know how I hate trying to keep secrets. Herself just ferrets them out. You'd be better not to tell me."

"I'll think on that." She patted his arm. For someone who tried so to be "proper," he was soft as new-fallen snow. Without him and Mrs. Hanson, she might not have survived her first year with her grandmother. She checked herself in the mirror above the hall table, tucked a strand of hair back in her snood, shook any remaining bits of melted snow off the hem of her skirt and headed for the library. A fire in the hearth had carried immense appeal at the moment.

"All right, what are you up to now?" Louise demanded after the greetings.

Arley sighed and shook her head. "Grandmother, it is nearing Christmas, if I need to remind you, and you have always said one shouldn't question other's secrets at Christmas."

"Humph." Her back straight as a lodgepole pine, Louise tipped her head slightly to peer over the top of her narrow glasses. "You know it is impolite to return one's words to the original speaker?"

Arley suppressed a smile, delighted to see a spark of gaiety in her grandmother's fading blue eyes. Even for one as serious and overwhelming as "Herself," as Hanson referred to her, of late she'd been rather sad or at least less stentorian than usual. Something had been bothering her, of that Arley was certain, but how to learn the cause put her at a loss. Direct questioning would get her nowhere.

"I've been to the orphanage to read, as I always do on Thursdays." She stood in front of the fire, warming first her hands, then her back.

"You should have stayed home in weather like this."

Cantankerous, that was a good description. "But I gave my word." She knew that would shut the old woman down. After all, a promise was a promise.

A knock came at the door. They turned to see Mrs. Hanson enter with a tea tray, which she set on the low table between the two leather wing chairs in front of the fireplace. "I brought your favorite, Miss Arley."

"Christmas tea?"

She nodded, the one curl that always sneaked out of her mobcap bobbing. "Mixed it myself."

"I *thought* I smelled drying orange peel." Arley lifted the lid on the teapot and inhaled the fragrance. "Ah, the perfumes of Christmas. I think one could welcome in the season just with them."

"And orange buns specially for you, ma'am." Mrs. Hanson indicated the snail-shaped buns with orange-flavored frosting, one of her specialties.

Louise nodded. "Thank you, Mrs. Hanson." Even though the couple had worked for her since shortly before Arley came to live there, Grandmother insisted they maintain formal relationships in speech and demeanor.

"Supper will be ready at six, or do you prefer six-thirty?"

"Six will be fine, thank you. Arley, will you pour?"

Arley caught the wink sent her way as Cook headed for the door. "Of course." Using the small server, she placed one of the buns on a plate and handed it with a napkin to her grandmother. Were Grandmother's hands shakier than usual? Arley watched without seeming to watch as she poured the tea, added one lump of sugar, set a spoon on the saucer and passed that across the low table.

Arley wasn't even sure when the shakiness had

started, for getting her grandmother to talk about anything as private as her personal health was like trying to dig a trench in the frozen Minnesota soil. She would most likely have to go behind her back again to talk with the doctor. Beauty was not something that had graced her grandmother, but the strong chin, wide brow and piercing eyes heralded strength beyond measure. Much of the laughter had left the mansion when her grandfather died ten years earlier, not that there had been an overabundance of hilarity even before then. A self-made man, astute in the ways of timber and finances, he'd built a fortune and encouraged his wife to take part in the business after their only son, Arley's father, left home to pursue his dream of teaching history as a professor at St. Olaf College in Northfield. He and his wife were on the train returning to the school when disaster struck. A bridge collapsed, dumping the train into a river and killing most of the passengers.

Five-year-old Arley had come to live with her grandparents immediately.

Surprised at the direction her thoughts were taking, Arley poured her own tea and bit into one of the buns, licking her fingers to get all the sweetness when she believed her grandmother wasn't looking.

"Arlayna, use your napkin."

"Yes, ma'am."

"So how were the children today?"

"Delightful as always. Little Nettie sure has carved herself a place in my heart."

"You know you should not get so attached. That can bring only heartache."

"But, Grandmother, how can I resist such a delightful child?" Arley knew better than to wait for an answer, so she added, "After all, it is nearly Christmas." She nibbled and sipped for a moment. "I'm thinking of doing something extra for the party at the orphanage. What if we provided a new piece of clothing for each of the children this year?" She'd almost slipped and mentioned the dollhouse. What was the matter with her?

"They haven't enough clothes? Surely the missionary societies will sponsor a clothing drive."

"But think how something brand-new would make them feel."

Louise shook her head. "That would not be helpful in the long run. They must learn to live within their means."

Arley sighed. "Would you like more tea?" At least she could provide hair ribbons. If only she had access to money of her own, what she could do to help those children… But while her grandmother felt she was being most generous with the allowance she gave Arley, she really had access to very little cash. Every penny of it would go into the dollhouse. When she heard the clink of a cup on a saucer, she glanced over at her grandmother.

"I think I will have a bit of a lie-down," Louise said, rising to her feet. "Please call me in half an hour."

"I will." This was another indication that there might be something wrong with her grandmother. She'd never taken naps before. "Are you all right?" The words sneaked past her resolve and hung on the air.

"Of course. Why? Whatever could be wrong?" Her eyebrows lowered at the same time as her shoulders straightened almost imperceptibly.

"Nothing. I just wondered."

"Ring Cook to pick up the tray."

"I will." Arley leaned over and poured herself the last of the tea. "In a bit. I'll enjoy the fire awhile longer."

"As you wish." The door closed with a snick behind her, a definite comment on her opinion of her grand-daughter's invasive question.

"Lord, how do I deal with her?" But only the gentle crack of a log crumbling in the fireplace answered her question. Sometimes she wondered if even *God* could soften her grandmother.

Chapter Six

❧

Nathan and Arley

Music. A violin played by someone with great skill.

Arley paused at the door to the wood-carver's shop. Surely it was coming from inside. She listened to the soaring of Handel's *Messiah,* her eyes burning from the beauty of it. When the overhead bell tinkled, the playing stopped.

Oh, please keep playing!

Lawrence Gunderson pushed back the curtain. "Good morning. You are out bright and early. But I have to tell you, the repairs on our wooden friend are not quite completed."

"That is no problem, I thought that might be so, but I have an entirely new idea I must talk over with you." She took a deep breath. "You play the violin so wonderfully."

He chuckled. "Thank you for the compliment, but that was my grandson."

"Oh." How could someone so grumpy play with such beauty? "No wonder he wants to make violins." She leaned slightly toward the old man. "My grandmother would love to hear him play."

"She always had a good ear and an appreciation for music. I'm glad to hear that has not changed."

"She did?" What other secrets did this man hold? She would love to know. Tucking the thought away to be pondered later, she tugged herself back on track. "I have a most wonderful idea, and I am hoping beyond hope that you can help me."

He nodded, his eyes twinkling. "If I can, I certainly would love to help make your idea a reality." He gestured to the curtain. "Perhaps we should discuss this over tea or coffee."

What a charming gentleman! And she'd get to see the Viking again. She mentally scolded herself for giving young Mr. Gunderson such a dime-novel title as she nodded her thanks and followed the wood-carver through the blue curtain.

"Here, let me take your cloak and you can hang your bonnet on the tree by the door. While I make the coffee, you tell me your idea. Nathan, do you want a cup, too?"

"I'll fix it." Nathan laid down the violin he'd been playing and nodded to Arley, who removed her gloves. "Good morning."

"Do you always play like that? I mean, every day?" So much for her manners, Arley thought. Grandmother was right, her tongue did get away with her at times, in spite of all the years of Grandmother's efforts to discipline her.

He paused on his way to the kitchen. "I try to."

"It was like hearing a bit of heaven."

She caught the rolling of his eyes. Couldn't he even accept a compliment? Boorish, that fit.

Lawrence motioned her to one chair and he took the other. "Now, while Nathan is busy with the coffee, tell me about your idea."

She told him about reading the book, the little girl's request, a brief mention of her childhood dream and ended with, "And so I wondered if you could build me a dollhouse for the orphanage. I would give it to them in my grandmother's name, which will be a surprise and part of my Christmas gift for her." She paused. Might as well tell him the rest. "And if you have time, I'd like to commission you to carve another nutcracker for her collection."

"Whew, that's a big order." He glanced at the calendar hanging above his workbench. "Three weeks until Christmas." He stroked his mustache with one finger. "What do you think, Nathan?"

"I think I have no idea what it would take to make a dollhouse and we have plenty of work here left to finish already." He poured water into the coffeepot and added coffee.

"Ah, but how do we disappoint a small child who has so little?"

Nathan shrugged as he walked to the door and let the cat back in. "Eugenia, your babies are restless."

The gray cat glanced up at him, chirped her answer and headed for the box by the stove. When she noticed Arley, she detoured and rubbed her head, then her back on Arley's skirt.

"She likes you," the senior Gunderson said.

"But she's only met me once." Arley stroked the cat's arched back.

"Doesn't matter. Cats know who to go to."

"Yes, she usually goes to people who don't like cats," Nathan said. "Perverse sense of humor."

Arley stared at the younger man in surprise. He'd actually sounded pleasant. She bent over to stroke the cat again, then watched as the animal crossed to her box and leaped in to care for her fussing babies. How wonderful it would be, Arley thought, to have a kitten of her own! But back to the business at hand.

"You would have to help us, you know," Lawrence said. At her look of confusion, the older man continued, "With all the decorating details, like walls and curtains and furnishings."

She gripped the chair arms in a moment of panic. How would she get away from home to do all that? But then, what fun it would be! Surely there must be bits and pieces of things around her grandmother's house that could be put to use. She nodded. "Of course." Somehow she would make it work—without lying. That would be the most difficult, but she'd learned that lesson years earlier. One did not lie to her grandmother. *Lord, I'm surely going to need Your help in this.*

"Good, then the three of us can begin immediately. Nathan, I commission you to start the drawings so we have a plan. Miss Dexter, you must describe to us the dollhouse you envision and I will search for wood scraps and things we can use to build it."

"Will you not need to buy supplies?" Arley asked.

He shook his head. "I have plenty of leftover lumber that needs to be used." He smiled his thanks as Nathan handed them each a cup of coffee. "Bring your drawing tools and let's gather around the table."

"But I…" Nathan shot a glance toward his workbench and the pieces of violin. His eyebrows drew together and he took a deep breath, obviously fighting with himself.

Arley watched the battle as the Viking smoothed out his face by some internal order and nodded. He set his coffee cup on the table and climbed the narrow stairs to an upper floor, returning instantly with a drawing board, straight edge, ruler and pencils.

His grandfather laid cookies on a plate and brought them to the table.

"I…I'm sorry, I never thought of the ramifications of all this," Arley said.

"Don't you go worrying about this. You just figure out a way to handle your grandmother." He smiled up at Nathan, who must have made sure no trace of a smile or any emotion leaked out.

How well he seems to know her. There's a mystery here, she thought.

As the discussion began on the project, Nathan made notes on the edges of the paper taped to his drawing board. Using her hands, Arley set the dimensions of the house as two stories, three-sided with bedrooms upstairs and all other living quarters downstairs. As she talked, she watched the outlines of the house flow from the tip of his pencil. The man was not only a musician and a woodworker, but an artist, as well.

"Will we have an attic for the help?" Mr. Gunderson inquired.

"I hadn't thought of that."

"With a roof of that pitch, there would be room for beds and dressers at least. Or pegs on the walls for clothes."

"So the stairwell would be used for all three floors, or wouldn't the stairs to the attic be at the end of the kitchen?" Nathan erased some lines and redrew them.

Arley watched the surety of the moves of his hands. He'd done architectural drawing before, obviously. Catching a glimpse of badly discolored and wrinkled skin when his cuff pulled back, she caught her breath. Had he been badly burned at one time? Her curiosity, always one of her stronger traits, made her want to know the story behind it. But her grandmother's continued admonitions to keep her nose in her own business won out.

Nathan flipped the page up, and before he could turn the next one, she saw his carefully drawn plans for a violin. Ignoring her response, he turned to the next blank sheet and took up his ruler again. He quickly laid out the front of the house, including potted trees on either side of the front door, on the steps.

"You've seen a dollhouse before?"

He nodded without looking up. "My youngest sister had one."

"And his father was not pleased," Lawrence said. "To put it mildly."

"His father is your son?"

"Yes."

Of course he was, you ninny. The names were the same. She bit down on her bottom lip as a reminder to keep her mouth closed. When the clocks all burst into chimes at the same moment, she stared up at the closest one. Noon. Where had the past three hours gone?

"I must get back home before they get suspicious." She pushed back her chair. "Thank you for your help."

"If you could stay for dinner, we could work this afternoon."

"Thank you, but I hadn't planned on being gone so long. Grandmother will…" She crossed to the coat tree and lifted down her blue bonnet, quickly setting it in place and tying the bow under her chin. As she reached for her cloak, the elder Mr. Gunderson took it from her and settled it around her shoulders.

"Bring what you can tomorrow to start decorating the interior of the rooms. I think we can have the walls and floors all in by then. How are you with needle and thread and a paintbrush?"

"Adequate. Do you think we can add a library by the parlor?" She pulled her gloves from a pocket. "Thank you again."

"Your nutcracker will be repaired and ready to take home tomorrow, also."

"Wonderful."

He walked her to the front door. "God bless." He stood waving as she hurried up the street. She looked back once to wave again, then took a run and slid on a patch of ice. She thought of ice-skating. She used to skate on the pond with the other children of the village and sometimes the adults, too. Did no one ever skate anymore, or had she just been left off the guest list? At her grandmother's instigation most likely.

She wondered if the Viking knew how to skate. Didn't every red-blooded Minnesotan, along with cross-country skiing and other winter activities? The thought of skating around the pond or lake, with him, her hand snug in a muff, made her face heat up in spite of the frigid air. Where had that thought come from?

Just in case her grandmother was watching, she reduced her pace to a more ladylike walk when she neared the front door of home. One would think that by her ancient age of twenty-five, she would be beyond such childish behavior.

"Herself has been looking for you," Hanson greeted her with a whisper and a check over his shoulder.

"I'm sorry. I lost track of time. But after we eat, I need to talk with you and Cook in the kitchen. I need your help."

"Anything I can do." He stood straight, as if saluting.

"There you are. We've been looking for you." Her grandmother stepped into the arched doorway.

Arley hung up her things. "Well, I've been out, but I'm here now and sorry I kept you from eating on time."

"Hanson is there to take your cloak and hang it up."

"Yes, Grandmother." Arley turned with a sigh and an apologetic glance at Hanson. He shouldn't get reprimanded because of her independent behavior. "Let me wash up and I'll join you."

"In the sunroom. We must take advantage of the light when we have it."

"What am I going to say to her?" Arley asked the

face in the mirror above the sink. When the idea hit her, she grinned and winked at herself. "Thank you, Father. You came through again."

After grace and with back straight and her napkin in her lap, Arley smiled at her grandmother. They were sitting at the round table in front of the window. "This is so much more pleasant than the dining room. Thank you for choosing to eat here." They both knew this was one of Arley's favorite rooms in the house.

"Where have you been all morning?" Nothing like a frontal attack.

"Now, Grandmother, must I remind you again about all the times you've told me not to ask questions around Christmas time."

"Humph."

"Did you have a good morning?"

"I was hoping you would write some letters for me."

That meant she would dictate and Arley would write as fast as possible. "Is there any reason we cannot do that this afternoon?'

"No, but we missed the post this way." She nodded to Hanson to set the soup dish on her plate.

Even with the sunshine streaming through the windows, there was a slight bite in the air, due, Arley knew, to her being gone without permission and without saying where. Had her grandmother had her way, she would have a rope or chain attached Arley's wrist and the other end attached to the chatelaine on the old woman's belt. The thought almost made Arley smile.

"This is good soup."

"Mrs. Hanson always makes good cream soups. It's a miracle this wasn't curdled, since you were so late."

It promised to be a long afternoon.

Chapter Seven

The cottage

"You sure you have everything, miss?" Henny fluttered around the basket.

"Well, as much as we could find. If you can think of somewhere else we can look…" Arley closed her eyes to reflect. She'd ransacked the sewing room, the linen closet, the trunks in the attic in search of bits of wallpaper and fabric. Never had she realized she could be so sneaky. Not only did she have to keep away from her grandmother, but from Mrs. Iverson, the housekeeper, who if she noticed anything amiss, would go directly to Louise.

In her basket Arley also had scissors, needle and thread, lamb's wool to use as stuffing for cushions and quilts, horsehair, leather from an old pair of gloves, string, embroidery thread, leftover yarn. She'd awakened this morning trying to decide how to create the doll family who would live in this house-to-be. If only she'd thought of this months ago, she could have ordered some of the things they couldn't make.

"You bundle up now," Mrs. Hanson ordered. "If the weather turns bad, I am sending the mister out for you."

Arley nodded. Right now, Mr. Hanson was busy taking her grandmother to a meeting at the church. She'd made noises about Arley accompanying her, but Arley had stood firm. When her grandmother started to argue, Arley gave her the look she'd practiced in the mirror. It was the sort of look her grandmother used to quell any opposition.

Louise Dexter left in a huff.

Arley set off for the woodworker's cottage, bundled up with a coat under her cloak and a scarf across the lower part of her face. The wind soughed through the naked tree branches, rattling some and snapping others with the cold. Clouds scudded across the eggshell-blue sky, playing follow-the-leader.

She paused at the door, hoping to hear the powerful violin music again, but the only sound was the sign overhead clattering in the wind. She pushed open the heavy door, and the bell announced her entry.

"Coming," she heard from the rear.

"It's only me." She moved to the blue curtain. "You needn't come out." She pushed the cloth aside and stepped into the other world, as she'd come to think of the living quarters. Her gaze zeroed in on the dollhouse on the workbench, bare walls inside and out and still roofless. A thrill skittered up her backbone. A dollhouse! They really were going to build one. She set her basket on the counter and crossed to the coat tree to hang up her outer garments, talking as she went. "I see you got started. I was afraid maybe you would change your mind."

"No, lass, a promise is a promise. But we have done the easy part. The details are what will eat up the time," Mr. Gunderson said.

She was about to inquire as to the whereabouts of his grandson when the back door opened and the man himself came in with flat sticks of cedar about an inch wide.

He held them up. "Shingles in the making." Setting his hat on the top of the tree, he nodded. "Good day, Miss Dexter." He actually smiled.

Her heart did a double thump and then skipped a beat. What a devastating smile! One thought scrambled after the other. Why didn't he use that smile more? Then, good thing he didn't. Most likely women fell all over themselves to get him to smile. What was his laugh like? *Get hold of yourself,* she commanded. Remember his scowl. That seems more the norm for him.

"Come over by the fire," Mr. Gunderson said, "and warm yourself. I'm surprised your grandmother let you walk over here in the cold."

Arley took the old man up on his offer. "She is using the buggy today, but Cook threatened that if it worsened, she'd send her husband after me."

"And your grandmother doesn't know you're here?" His gray eyebrows rose on the question, making deep wrinkles in his wide forehead.

"No, but she won't ask. I warned her about questions at Christmas, as she does to me all the time."

Lawrence's cheeks rounded with his grin. "Got one back at her, did you?"

Arley nodded, then crossed to the stove to peek into the box of cat and sleeping kittens. Eugenia yawned, her pink tongue curling around white needle teeth, and closed her eyes. The kittens had seemed to grow overnight.

Mr. Gunderson pointed out a kitten. "I'm reserving the one with the white feet for you."

Desire overrode common sense. "Oh, I hope so."

The sound of a saw drew her attention to the workbench where Nathan had clamped the cedar sticks into a vise and was now cutting them into one-and-a-half-inch pieces with a fine-bladed saw.

"How about I bring the dollhouse over here to the kitchen table and you can work on the interior while I start on furniture?"

"That would be perfect." She went to fetch her basket and saw the neck of the violin lying beside the body now ready for the top to be glued in place. The grain of the wood glowed in the light. "That—your violin will be beautiful."

He glanced up from his concentration on the saw. "It is coming along."

"Would you consider playing sometime for my grandmother? She loves music of any kind, but the violin especially."

"We'll see." He set another cluster in the clamp, measured and started sawing again.

Back to being a man of very few words.

She shrugged and took her basket to the table. "What

colors do you think would do well on the outside walls?"

"Gray with navy, burgundy and cream trim," Nathan replied for his grandfather.

"He's the artist," Lawrence said. "I'm just a wood-carver and worker."

Arley motioned toward the front showroom. "With all that beautiful work, you are not an artist?"

"Only in wood. You don't see paint and painted trims out there. I can put any kind of a clear finish on wood, but when it comes to colors—" he leaned forward and lowered his voice "—I'm partially color-blind, not in all colors, but don't ask me to match anything in dark colors."

Arley shook her head. "How do you paint the nut-crackers, then?"

"They better be accurate on the paint labels is all I got to say." He held up several small pieces of dark wood. "Now, this will become a bed in a few minutes, and your nutcracker is good as new."

"Thank you." She thought to retrieve her reticule, tucked in the pocket of her coat. But she'd not put any cash in there before leaving home. "You must tell me how much I owe you so I can bring it tomorrow."

"We'll discuss that later." He fitted the pieces together, and they indeed made a bed with both head- and footboard. "Now, I can also glue little bits of gin-gerbread trim onto the gable ends of the roof, like all the fancy work on your grandmother's porch." He opened a pot of glue, and, using a tiny sliver of wood, dabbed some on the joints of his creation. "That's the second bed. How many do you think we need?"

"Three, one for each bedroom. The fourth room upstairs will make a nice sewing room. I have ticking in here to make the mattresses." Piece by piece she removed the supplies from her basket, laying them on the table in color groups. "I didn't bring flour to make wallpaper paste."

"In that canister." He nodded toward the shelves on the wall.

Arley used her ruler to measure the rooms and decided to work on the master bedroom first. She unrolled a strip of cream-colored wallpaper and held it up to the rooms, deciding to cover all the ceilings on the main floor with it. After cutting the pieces she tested each one against the space and nodded. Using a fork, she mixed flour and water to a thick paste and returned to the table.

"There are brushes over there on the workbench. Use one of the worn ones."

Nathan handed her a brush just as she reached the bench.

"Thank you." She paused to watch him. The frame of the roof was finished and covered with a thin board, and now he was gluing the shingles into place, one by one, starting with the row along the eaves, just as one would with a real house. Real shingles. She wanted to clap her hands and spin in place as she used to when a child. "I never dreamed this would have such detail!"

"We thought of painting the roof, but then grandfather had this idea. It does look rather well, doesn't it?"

"What are those squares for?" She pointed to several places drawn on the board. In the process, her arm brushed his. The current that jumped between them made her step back. "Excuse me, I—"

"Dormers and a chimney." He continued painting glue on the end of the shingle and setting it perfectly in place. "We haven't decided for sure on the dormers. Depends on the time. Have you thought about glass for the windows?"

Must have been the carpets, she thought, and the sparks caused by friction. She and the neighbor boys used to rub their feet on the rugs in the winter and try to sting each other. Surely that was what it was. He obviously did not feel a thing. She took the brush and returned to her chair, where she smoothed paste onto the ceiling and a light coat on the paper, then pressed the paper into place, carefully smoothing out the lumps and bubbles.

"That looks perfect. One would think you did this every day." Lawrence came around the table to her side. With the house resting on its front, she was able to do the ceilings more easily.

Sometime later she came out of her concentration to hear the wind whistling around the corners of the house. It had picked up. Should she leave now or wait for Hanson to come?

Lawrence stuck more wood in the stove and pulled a kettle, which had been sending out tantalizing smells, to the hotter part of the stove. "Soup will be ready soon. I thought we'd eat in front of the fireplace so we don't have to clear the table."

"I should be getting home."

"Not in this wind. Hanson will come. You keep working. Doing too good a job to stop now."

Arley stared at the older man. Too many compliments. She wasn't used to that. She started to respond but had to swallow twice and clear her throat before she could get the thank-you out. She half smiled at his quizzical look, then stepped back ostensibly to study her decorating skills, but in reality to get control of the emotions that threatened to swamp her. She'd finished the ceilings and used striped silk for the upper walls of the dining room. The bottom half needed wainscoting. The parlor sported a burgundy calico with tiny dots and the master bedroom a gold silk. She'd used red-and-white gingham on the kitchen walls and made a braided rug from the same fabric for the floor.

Nathan crossed to stand beside her, wiping any remaining glue from his hands with a rag. "You've done a lot. Looks nice."

Arley wanted to take a step, no, several steps back. He seemed to suck all the air out around him. Why all of a sudden was he saying nice things? Kind words didn't fit the image she had of him at all. A few days ago she'd yelled at him and today, between him and his grandfather, she was nearly on the verge of tears. She who never cried, who had sworn off crying over such a silly thing as hurt feelings years ago. Her grandmother's training had taken hold and taken hold well.

"Th-thank you." Her breath came out on a *whoosh*. "I…I better clean up my mess."

"No, leave it. As Grandpa said, we'll eat in front of the fire. Much warmer."

The last thing Arley needed to be at the moment was warmer. What was the matter with her? Think of something to get a conversation going, she ordered herself. Surely all those lessons in deportment could come in handy about now. Family—that should be a safe topic. "Do you have any brothers and sisters?" she asked.

"Two sisters, one older, one younger."

At least he'd answered. "Where are you from?" Would he think her nosy? Didn't he know anything about keeping a conversation going? It was his turn to add more or ask a question.

"Minneapolis."

"Life here must seem strange after living there." She sorted through her bits of fabric, looking for the perfect piece.

"It is quiet and I needed that."

Finally he'd offered something personal. She waited, hoping he would continue. Glancing up, she saw the old man smiling at her. His nod gave her a feeling she was on the right track. "It that why you play your violin?"

"To destroy the quiet, or…?" He glued another piece in place before looking over his shoulder. "I would rather play the violin than just about anything else."

"You play beautifully. I wanted to stand outside and just listen."

Nathan nodded. "And you wouldn't have to stand outside."

Was that a smile that almost touched his eyes? She smiled back and nodded.

The jingling of harness bells could be heard over the rush of the wind. Surely it was Mr. Hanson come to fetch her. A rap at the door and the tinkle of the bell came almost simultaneously.

"Hello, anyone here?" Hanson's voice.

Nathan crossed to the curtain and pulled it aside. "Come on back and stand by the fire. We were just about to have dinner."

Arley headed for the coat tree to get her things. They couldn't leave the horses out in weather like this for long. She introduced the Gundersons to Hanson.

"Can you stay long enough for a bowl of soup?" the elder Gunderson asked as he led the driver closer to the fire.

"Thank you, but I think this storm is going to get worse, and we'd better get home before it does." Hanson glanced around the room, his gaze landing on the dollhouse, now upright again on the table. "Is this the secret project?" Leaving the fire, he moved to the table. "How clever!" He peered into each room and studied the pieces of furniture, some in various stages of construction. "How will you get all this done in—" he paused to count the days "—less than two weeks before the party at the orphanage?"

"That's why I need to work here every moment I can," Arley said.

"Without Herself getting wind of it?" The man shook his head. "Ah, Miss Arley, she is too sharp for that. She'll ferret it out of you some way."

Surprisingly, Nathan looked at Hanson and asked, "You have any suggestions?"

"Perhaps some of the rest of us could help with the furnishings," Hanson replied. "I've always been a fair hand at carving, and the missus can wield a needle with the best of them. Especially if this storm tucks us all in for a few days." He hesitated. "Would extra help be all right with you?"

"Of course, of course." Lawrence stroked his mustache as he pondered. "How about you make the cabinets for the kitchen?" He showed the measurements with his fingers. "About this long and this high."

"With brads for knobs?" Hanson asked.

"Good idea."

Arley finished buttoning her coat and settled her bonnet on her head. "I must remember to take the nutcracker."

"Oh, yes." Nathan retrieved the box from the workbench. "You'd never know he'd been wounded." When he handed it to her, his fingers brushed hers. His eyes widened slightly. "I packed it carefully."

For some reason, her gaze refused to leave his face, no matter how much she blinked. "I, ah, thank you." She took the box and this time did back up. Fleeing was a good alternative to drowning in the pools that were the blue of his eyes.

"I…I'll see you tomorrow…if the weather permits." Her voice sounded strange, even to her own ears. Husky, as if she had a sore throat. Only she'd felt just fine—up to that moment.

"Yes," Nathan said. But the smile had left his voice, leaving the grumpiness before.

"Men," she muttered to herself as Mr. Hanson tucked the heavy robes around her in the sleigh. Whatever had possessed her back there?

Chapter Eight

Nathan and Arley

"Shame she had to leave so abruptly."

Nathan looked up from his soup and took a bite of his buttered bread. "Yes. We were coming along well on it."

"Delightful young lady." Lawrence stared out the window. "Shame Louise has been so hard on her."

"Louise. Thou darest call the queen by her given name?"

Lawrence shook his head, his eyes twinkling above rosy cheeks. "I knew her long before she assumed the throne."

"I feel there is a story there."

"Many stories." The old man's eyes left off delight and wandered faraway pastures, not all of them sunny, from the look on his face. "We met in church, which was the social center, too. That, and the schoolhouse.

When we grew old enough for schooldays at our one-room school, Louise was never short on ideas, some good and some that got us all into trouble. One of our teachers left in the middle of the year, due to, as the story goes, such willful children."

"You, willful?"

"Hopefully age and experience bring on the wisdom the Bible promises. I asked for that many times through the years. Pleaded, in fact." He set down his soup bowl and picked up his coffee cup, cradling it between fingers scarred by the knives and splinters. "I thank God daily for His bountiful answers to prayer."

Why did he get the feeling, Nathan pondered, that there'd been something between his grandfather and Louise? Might as well take the bull by the horns, as his grandfather often said. "Did you fall in love with her?"

Lawrence shook his head. "No, I didn't fall in love with her. I loved her from the first and it just grew through the years."

"So what happened? You married Grandmother and had my father."

Lawrence got up and threw more wood on the fire. "We better get back to our labors here. If you'd rather spend the afternoon on your violin, I understand."

Nathan gathered up the dishes and set them in the sink. There'd be no more reminiscences today, of that he was certain, but what he'd heard had sure stoked his curiosity.

"Think I'll see if I can't get that roof done first," Lawrence said. "Would hate to lose some of those pieces."

"I'll bring the cedar in," Nathan offered. "And fill up the wood box while I'm at it." While they stored much of the cured hardwood upstairs on storage racks where the air was the driest, a shed outside held more, along with firewood Nathan had spent hours splitting while his burned body healed. Using the injured back muscles had kept them strong and limber in spite of the doctor's predictions that he'd make them worse. The labor had also healed his mind, driving out the fury, sending it into the wood rather than letting it eat away at him. In spite of his mother's pleas, he'd known that he'd find healing at his grandfather's house and not at home, where his father told everyone how many times a day to breathe. It sounded as if his father and Arlene's grandmother Louise had a lot in common. How a gentle man like his grandfather had raised a son like Nathan's father was beyond him. Had his father listened to the suggestions of his superintendent, the explosion might never have happened. He knew for certain that if he returned to work, he and his father would be fighting constantly. It wasn't worth it.

By the time he'd brought in all the wood, his lungs burned from the cold. Most likely it would get below zero this night, if it hadn't already. The wind sucked up the snowflakes and compressed them into stinging ice pellets.

"Thank you, Mr. Hanson. I'm grateful I didn't try to walk home in that." Arley had set the boxed nutcracker in her basket and laid a cloth over the trappings needed for the dollhouse rooms. She'd brought it all back with her since there was a real possibility that they'd be house-bound by morning. Surely she could hide out in the sewing room, and perhaps Henny would like to help, too. If they could stay away from the housekeeper, Mrs. Iverson.

Entering the house through the kitchen door seemed much safer. Besides, it was closer to the carriage house, where the horses were stabled. In former days of glory, when her grandfather was still alive, there had indeed been a carriage out there, along with buggies and sleighs and a wagon for hauling things out behind. The big wagon was still there, the iron wheels rusting into the ground because they weren't being used. Her grandmother had sold the carriage and all but one buggy, a sleigh and a horsecart. Traveling on the train was far easier than using the carriage. Her grandmother deplored wasting money.

"Get in here before you catch your death." Mrs. Hanson bustled around, taking Arley's cloak first, then scarf and coat, and draping them over a chair.

Arley laughed. She felt just as she had when she was little and had been out playing in the snow with the other children of Willow Creek. "I think we just stepped back fifteen years or more in time." She dropped a kiss on Mrs. Hanson's plump cheek. "*Mange takk.*" All those friends of hers were married now, or had moved away. But then, when did she have time for friends, other than social calls, anyway?

"Get on with you." Cook peered at the basket and whispered, "Did you get it?"

"Yes, why?"

"She's been looking for it, said her favorite was missing."

Arley heaved a sigh. "Just in time. I'll go put it out now." She removed the box from the basket, opened it and unwrapped the nutcracker, checking carefully for any signs of the accident. None. The soldier looked good as new—in fact better, since he'd received a good rubbing and perhaps a coat of wax. She sniffed. Sure enough. She should probably do the same for the rest of the collection to help them remain in good condition.

"Do you know where she is?"

"Up in her room, said she was going for a bit of a lie-down."

"How long ago?"

Cook looked at the clock. "Maybe half an hour."

"Good." Arley held the nutcracker in one hand and pushed open the door to the butler's pantry that led into the dining room. She'd put this one right in the middle, where it usually stood.

She had laid the nutcracker on his side for safety's sake while she'd moved the others around to give this one room. Glancing back, she noticed two initials were carved in the base. L.G. Lawrence Gunderson. Had he made this for her grandmother years before? She recalled the look in his eyes when he'd removed the broken pieces of it from the box. He'd remembered but not said a thing. Were they good memories or bad? Shaking her head, she set the nutcracker in the place of honor.

"There you are. I've been looking for you."

Arley fumbled to keep from knocking another figure

over at the sound of her grandmother's voice. Then, with all the nutcrackers secure, she turned to smile at the woman coming through the door.

"What were you doing?"

"Just rearranging the nutcrackers. I've been taking them into the kitchen one at a time for a good polishing."

"Oh, I knew_ one was missing." Louise peered through her glasses at those on the buffet. "There he is."

Lord, that was just a very tiny white lie, surely not enough to worry about. And I am going to polish them all now.

Louise turned and stared at her granddaughter. "Where have you been? I was getting worried."

"Now, remember what I said…"

"I know what you said. But you could at least tell me when you are going to be gone. I had some things for you to do."

"Perhaps I can do them now, or at least I can make a list." Arley took her grandmother's arm. "Let's go into the library and have Henny bring us in some tea and cookies. I think I'll have a sandwich, too. What about you?"

"No, cookies and tea will be fine. You wouldn't be willing to read to me for a bit, I don't suppose."

Arley thought of her basket and the curtains for the dollhouse parlor she wanted to make out of the red velvet leftovers from a dress she'd had years ago. On the way home in the sleigh, she'd figured out how to make gold tassels from embroidery thread. "Of course I'll read to you." She could always make the tassels after her grandmother went to bed. "And, Grandmother, I would love to hear some of the stories of when you were growing up. It's been a long time since you've told me any. Especially stories of Christmas."

"You have to remember," Louise said after they were seated and served, "we didn't live like we do here. My father owned the general store in town and my mother helped him as much as she could, while raising their five children."

"And you were the oldest?"

"So I helped at the store. That's where I learned so much about business." She paused for a moment, looking back. "One Christmas when I was little— Willow Creek was hardly even a village then—I wanted a real doll, not a doll made from scraps like my mother had made for me. I must have seen a picture of one." She shook her head. "Funny, since I don't remember playing much with the doll I had. As the eldest, I helped with the new baby. I guess dressing him was like dressing a doll. Selmer was a good baby."

"Did you ever get the doll?"

"Oh, no. There was no money for such extravagance. But I did get new hair ribbons and a shiny little mirror. I wonder what happened to the mirror? But thanks to my father and his trading with Indians, we all received beaded deerskin moccasins that year. I think all five of us wore those until they fell apart in spite of the patches." She gazed into the fire. "Will you read now?"

As she flipped to the book marker, Arley felt like crying. She'd never heard that story before.

Much later, when Arley finally headed for bed after

working on furnishings, dollhouse-size, she parted the heavy draperies over the window of her room so she could look out. Swirling snow hid the Christmas star. She sighed and let the draperies fall back. Ice on the window made her grateful for the warmth coming up through the floor radiator. Were Nathan and his grandfather warm enough in their log cabin? He'd offered to have him play his violin just for her. The thought made her spirit soar. "Soon" wouldn't be soon enough.

Chapter Nine

Nathan and Arley

"'P ears to me you're worrying about something."

Nathan glanced over at the table where his grandfather was carving spindles for the porch railing. "What makes you think that?"

"Two things—the frown wrinkling your forehead and the pile of shavings."

Nathan looked down, then at the piece of wood still in his hands. If a customer wanted to buy a toothpick, he had done a mighty fine job of making one.

"Thought you might like to talk about it. Always helps."

Nathan considered where his thoughts had been and decided he might as well talk. Discussing things with his grandfather had worked before, surely it could work again. After all, his grandfather knew his father well, better than Nathan did.

"I'm dreading the letter that I know will be coming any day now." He blew out a breath.

"Take no worry for the morrow. A day's own troubles are sufficient for the day. That's a bit of a paraphrase, but the wisdom is there."

"Easier said than done." Nathan snapped the toothpick between thumb and forefinger, then dropped it into the shavings pile.

"Have you a plan?"

"Vaguely." Nathan tipped his head back and gazed at the ceiling. "I don't want to go back. The thought of living in the cities again, going to work every day in that office—with him, doing what he orders even when I violently disagree—making money hand over fist…"

"Making money is not such a bad thing."

"No, it's not. But doing so on the backs of others less fortunate and not giving them adequate recompense or even a modicum of politeness—I can't do it anymore."

"Can't?"

"Can't and won't. He will never understand that." Nathan stared at the old man. "Where did all his drive, selfishness come from? Look at you. Why can't he be more like you?"

"God hasn't had time to soften his heart yet."

"Meaning?"

"My son has always done well for himself. His mother pushed him to succeed, and between them they were quite a pair. She always wanted more and she ingrained that way of living in him. When she died, he decided to honor her memory by continuing in the same vein and becoming highly successful."

"But what about you? Why are you so different?"

"Heartbreak can change a man."

"When your daughter died?" His father had told him about the little sister who'd died of typhoid when his mother did, along with a baby son and half the town. His father had been away at school and missed the epidemic.

"I found that Jesus himself is the only solace. I could become bitter…"

"Like my father?"

"Or I could let the good Lord heal me and lead me in whatever direction He chose."

"Well, the peace you learned is why I came to live with you. I believed this was my only chance." Nathan glanced toward the workbench. "Music has been my surcease for many years. You know how I dreamed of becoming a concert violinist…" His sigh echoed in the quiet room. "Might have made it, but we'll never know. And now I feel I might have a second chance, at life, anyway. My father wants to take that away from me according to his way, which he thinks is best. He's given me one year to recover and return." Nathan paused, thinking back on the conversation with his father when he was struggling to recuperate. His father had said he would keep the position open until the end of the year, which was fast approaching.

"So what good is worrying about this doing you?" Lawrence said.

"None whatsoever. In fact it's giving me a headache." Nathan set his knife on the arm of the chair and stood to stretch both arms above his head, his fingertips touching the ceiling. "Give me one of those pieces of wood and I promise to make a porch post, not another toothpick. Then I'll play for a while if that's all right with you."

"Listening to you play is more than all right with me."

"Do you think Miss Dexter plays the piano?"

"Most likely. Her grandmother would have insisted she learn all the appropriate social graces. As for her skill, you would have to hear her play."

"She says what she thinks—surely that didn't come by training." Most women he knew did everything they could to be agreeable, at least on the surface. How refreshing it was to talk with a woman who was not afraid to express her thoughts. Not that he appreciated the tongue-lashing he'd received that first day, no matter how much he deserved it. "Do you suppose she has any idea who I really am? I mean, we are well known in the cities."

"I doubt it. I don't believe her grandmother knows she has come here, though if she did, Louise would put two and two together."

"And get five. I'm not that man any longer." Not that Nathan was certain deep inside that he ever was the socialite people expected. He hoped and prayed he took more after his grandfather than his father.

The storm started up again about the same time Nathan picked up his violin. It was hard to say which sang more fortissimo.

Arley had awakened more than once to the sound of the wind, but it had blown itself out by morning. When she tried to look out, she had to scrape the ice off the window first. The rising sun set the frost fronds on the glass to sparkling. Arley watched, entranced, as sun fire danced from crystal to crystal. How could a storm that sounded so evil leave such beauty behind? Shivering in spite of her flannel nightdress, she hurried behind her screen to don long johns, wool stockings that came to her knees, an underpetticoat, a heavy quilted wool petticoat, an overpetticoat and her wool serge skirt. Grateful for the heat blowing up the vent, in spite of the edict not to start the big coal furnace down in the basement until the sun was up, Arley reminded herself to thank Mr. Hanson for warm air and warm water. While her grandmother was one of the first in town to install running water with a water heater in her home, she hated to use expensive coal to excess.

With her hair brushed and bundled into a snood, Arley tiptoed past her grandmother's door and made her way downstairs to the one room that was always cozy—the kitchen.

"Cold enough for you?" Mr. Hanson raised his coffee cup in greeting.

"Thank you for warming early. At least it is not snowing." Arley glanced out the window. "Perhaps I should ski over to Mr. Gunderson's shop."

"Herself would have my head if I allowed you to do such a thing. Are you sure it wouldn't be best to remain in the house today? She is getting mighty curious." He smiled up at his wife as she refilled his coffee cup. *"Takk."* While the Hansons spoke Norwegian and had taught Arley to speak it, too, they rarely used it around others. Another decree from her grandmother, although she'd learned the language as a child, too. Most everyone in Willow Creek was of Norwegian descent, at least the older families.

"The cinnamon buns are ready."

"Oh, yes, please. I could tell you were baking from the moment I awoke." She gazed down at the perfectly formed roll with icing dribbling down the sides. "You are an artist with all things edible. Not that your sewing skills are anything to sneeze at, either."

Mrs. Hanson pulled a basket off a shelf and set it in front of Arley. "Wish we had started earlier on this, but I'll do more this evening."

Arley lifted out a miniature velvet quilt, navy, with the squares stitched in white and white trim around the edges. "For the master bedroom?"

"*Ja,* and curtains to match. I have a rug started."

Then Mr. Hanson set out several miniature cabinets, some with countertops, but all with carved doors and brads set for handles. "For the kitchen. I have a chest of drawers about done for the bedroom."

"Oh, I can't tell you how pleased I am! Did you never sleep last night?"

"Ah, what with the wind howling like a banshee, sleep would have been impossible, anyway, you know?"

Arley finished her roll and wiped her mouth with a napkin. "Delicious as always. When Grandmother rings, I'll take her tray up. Maybe that will help calm her curiosity."

When Arley left in the sleigh sometime later, her one basket had overflowed into another, this one holding finished products.

The snow on the steps to the door of the shop had been shoveled and swept when Arley arrived. Hanson helped her out of the sleigh and carried one of the baskets for her, then pushed open the heavy door.

"There you go, miss. I'll fetch you about two. And no ideas of walking, you hear me?"

"Yes, sir." Her grandmother wasn't the only stubborn person in the Dexter household. "It's *me!*" she called, stomping her feet on the mat to get rid of the snow as Hanson shut the door behind them.

"Come on back," Mr. Gunderson said, holding back the curtain. "Feels like I better add some wood to that stove, too. Not much chance of customers, but they'll stay longer if they're not freezing."

"Wait until you see what we have," Arley said. She stopped with a gasp at the entrance to the workroom. The dollhouse. The roof and dormers were in place, along with a cunning chimney that looked like real brick. "Oh, how perfect!" She looked to the two Gunderson men. "I take it there wasn't a lot of sleep going on here, either." When they started to make excuses, she raised a hand. "I know, the storm was too noisy to sleep."

Lawrence chuckled as he set the baskets on the table. "The older one gets, the less sleep one needs."

Arley turned from hanging up her things. "Mrs. Hanson sent some buns and bread along." She dug in the basket. "And jam. I hope you don't mind."

"Not at all." The older man added wood to the stove. "So today you will stay for dinner?"

"Hanson's coming back to get me at two."

"Indeed I am," Hanson said.

"Good, good," Lawrence said. He picked up the cabinets and held them to the light. "How perfect. We'll install them today."

Eugenia rubbed against Arley's skirt and greeted her with a chipper meow.

"Well, look at that." Nathan nodded at the cat. "You are indeed a member of the family now."

"Mr. Hanson, you must look in the box." Arley crossed to the wooden crate. She leaned over and picked up the white-footed kitten, cuddling it in her two hands. "Isn't he the cutest?"

Hanson ran a gentle finger over the tiny head. "Look, his eyes are opening."

The kitten yawned, showing pink tongue and minute needle teeth. He squirmed and Arley put him back with the others, who immediately set up a kitten chorus demanding their mother return.

Nathan smiled at Arley. "See what you started?" His gaze held hers. "I'd better get back to small pieces."

"Poor Eugenia, never a moment's peace with four young'uns." Mr. Gunderson followed the cat to the door and let her outside. "Well, let's get at it. I already mixed some paste for the wall coverings. I'll keep working on the porch pieces and Nathan has promised us siding."

"Siding? Can't we just paint the outside?" She ignored the chuckle from the workbench.

"I'll return later." Hanson tipped his hat. "Keep up the good work."

Arley stared at the dollhouse. "I thought of turning

the red-and-white gingham on the diagonal for wallpaper in the kitchen."

Mr. Gunderson nodded. No response from the workbench.

She cut fabric to fit and smeared the paste on the wall, smoothing out little lumps of flour with her fingertips.

"Here, let me help." Lawrence removed the roof and together they tipped the house on its front. "Good thing we haven't added the porch yet. I hadn't thought of that."

"I did." Nathan was paying attention to the conversation after all.

Arley nodded toward the workbench and sent the older man a questioning look. He shrugged. Arley shook her head. Light and dark, that was Nathan. She decided to ignore him and focus on the job at hand.

"That's crooked."

The male voice over her shoulder made her jump. "Bad bugs! Couldn't you have warned me?"

"It wasn't like I snuck up on you." Nathan's voice bore a hint of laughter. "Bad bugs?"

It *was* laughter, she could see it in his eyes.

"If my grandmother had raised you, you would have learned early on the folly of swearing or speaking crudely."

"The bar-of-soap treatment?"

"Yes, it was quite effective." She returned to straighten the fabric wallpaper while it was still wet enough to do so. "She always said that intelligent people did not need to swear."

"Sometimes knowing a foreign language is helpful."

He used the turpentine rag to work glue off his fingers. The smell of turpentine was imbedded in the very walls, she was sure.

"You swear in foreign languages?"

"If necessary." He left her to throw another log in the fireplace.

She felt a cool draft against her neck. It seemed to come from the spot where he'd been standing. Had she sensed his presence even before he'd spoken? What a silly thought!

When he came back, he took a chair across the table and picked up a carving knife. He made one cut and set it down again, a small sound of disgust accompanying the action.

"Bad bugs?" she said, glancing up at him.

"Not quite. Just need to sharpen this again." He stood. "Grandpa, you have anything that needs sharpening?"

"Yes, thank you." His grandfather held up several carving tools. "Even pine and cedar take the edge off quickly."

So, Mr. Nathan Gunderson, tell me about your siblings, she considered asking. Was that intrusive? What could she use to start a conversation? *What did you do before you came to Willow Creek?* Somehow she had an idea he did not want to talk about his former life. Since politics and religion were hardly safe topics and he'd gone into his own world again, she left that and focused instead on the dollhouse kitchen. Now the diagonal on the other wall did not match the first two. She took it off and tried again.

With a frown, she pushed back her chair and walked around the table.

"Can I help you?" Lawrence asked gently.

"I...I'm not sure. Will there be trim around the window holes?" She crossed her arms and tapped her chin with one finger. "It just doesn't look quite right."

"Why not use plain white on that wall?" Nathan said. "You are going to make the curtains out of the plaid, too, right?" He had left off smoothing the tools on the whetstone and come up behind her again. "A bit jumpy, aren't you?"

"Well, if you would quit sneaking up on me..." She turned to glare at him, but found him so close she bumped him with her elbow. The contact made her swallow. Bad bugs. She was getting as grouchy as he was and it was all his fault.

"Sor-ry." He returned to his sharpening. His grandfather wiggled his eyebrows at her and she plunked herself back in the chair to rip the gingham off the wall.

"And it's gingham, not plaid," she said with a tad more force than necessary.

"Looks plaid to me," Nathan returned.

She ignored him. Eugenia jumped up on the table and walked around inspecting the dollhouse. She sniffed the walls and batted at a string hanging from the upper floor, then sat in the square of sunlight and proceeded to give herself a bath.

Arley watched her, entranced by the light glinting off the fluffy gray fur, the care with which the cat licked her paws and swiped her face and ears. The end of Eugenia's tail twitched in rhythm with her coarse tongue. "You are so beautiful," Arley said.

How could her grandmother call cats dirty? The description didn't fit, not with all the care cats took to keep their fur clean. She'd watched the mother cat clean her babies, not always to their delight. What would it take to get her grandmother's agreement for her to have the gray kitten? What would she name it? Three white boots, a pink nose with white around it in a stripe up the forehead. At bit of white on his chest. All the rest, gray fluff, like his mother.

Eugenia finished her ablutions and strolled over to bump Arley's hand. When she sat back in her chair, the cat jumped down in her lap and, purring loud as a train engine, curled into a ball and promptly fell asleep. Arley stroked her back and the purr deepened. The vibrations soaked through the layers of her skirts and warmed her legs. How could one cat emit so much heat?

"Do you need help?" Mr. Gunderson asked.

"No, but I can't work with her on my lap."

"Put her down then," Nathan suggested. His chuckle said he'd come back to join them again.

"But she's sleeping."

"Cats are opportunists. If they find a comfortable lap, they take advantage." Mr. Gunderson rose and picked up the cat, setting her on the chair he'd just left.

Maybe that was something she'd missed in her growing-up years. A comfortable lap to take advantage of. Maybe a cat on the lap with a soothing purr was what her grandmother needed.

Chapter Ten

The cottage and Sunday church

She could hear him playing just after she crossed the bridge. The notes kissed her ears and warmed her heart. How could a man who played like he did not be carried out of his sadness, for she had thought it that. But perhaps it was bitterness. Well, she knew the result of bitterness; she lived with it every day, though try as she might, she could not understand what her grandmother was bitter about. Yes, her husband had died far too young, but other widows were able to go about their lives without a cloud hanging over their heads. Standing there, enjoying the sun and the music, she thought of her grandmother and the mystery of her and Mr. Gunderson. Surely there had been feelings there. What had happened?

She paused when the notes dropped to a pianissimo too soft to penetrate beyond the walls. But when they soared again, she smiled and walked to the door. If only she'd had the talent to go along with all the hours she'd spent at the piano. She could play well enough for people to sing along, but not with the heart a true musician could pour into the effort. Like this violinist.

She pushed open the door and the music stopped as if connected to the tinkling bell. "Why do you stop playing when I come?" she asked as she crossed the showroom floor to the blue curtain.

"I wasn't sure it was you." Nathan was putting the violin back in the case.

"Shall I announce myself with a special rap?" She shrugged, as her words had more than a hint of pepper to them.

"Would you like me to continue?" He held the bow, ready to loosen the tautness by twisting the screw at one end.

"Yes, if you please." She hung her things on the tree. "Where is your grandfather?"

"He went to pick up a package at the depot. He said he'd be right back." Nathan settled the violin against his shoulder. "Is there anything special you would like to hear?"

"You were playing Handel's *Messiah* one day. I would love to hear that again." She crossed to look into the kitten kingdom. All were sprawled, tummies rounded, smiles on their faces. Eugenia greeted her from the hearth, where she lay with her front feet folded under her chest, her green eyes blinking. As soon as Arley stroked her back, the purr joined the music flowing from the instrument again. Arley joined the cat on the raised stone hearth, the better to watch Nathan play, for it was also a visual delight.

He played the violin with his entire body. Eyes closed, he swayed to the rhythm, his bowing arm strong and limber so the bow brought rich and vibrant notes from the strings. His fingers danced on the strings, flashing faster than the eye could see as the tempo soared, singing the hallelujahs straight to heaven. "For the Lord God omnipotent reigneth…"

Her mind formed the words as her eyes closed. Hallelujah. She felt the burn of tears behind her lids. How could one help but cry at the incredible beauty of the music? She knew she had come to work on the dollhouse, but how could she do anything but worship?

Her God, the music.

Her eyes fluttered open. She felt like a giant bud was growing within her and bursting into bloom with the music, welling up with joy unlike anything she'd ever experienced. Oh, the power in music.

She peered through her lashes to make sure he wasn't watching her. Eyes closed, he appeared still lost in the music. She breathed a sigh of relief and schooled herself back into Arley, ordinary Arley, sitting on the hearth, stroking a purring cat who had crawled into her lap and thinking on what next to do on the dollhouse.

"Wonderful, counselor, almighty God the everlasting Father, the Prince of Peace." The words would not leave her.

"Wonderful!" Mr. Gunderson pushed open the back door, interrupting her reverie, and set the box he was carrying on the bench by the door. "Ah, I see you made it, Miss Dexter. What do you think of our efforts?"

Eugenia leaped from her lap, creating a cooling of the warm comfort she'd shared with Arley. She dashed out the door before it closed, making Mr. Gunderson laugh.

Nathan ended his playing and laid the violin in its case, releasing the tension on the bow and clipping it to the lid. "And all is well?"

"Yes, and glorious to come home to such a concert." He hung up his things and stopped at the table where the dollhouse stood, the exterior ready for paint.

"The porch is beautiful," she said with a smile. *Nathan's beautiful, when he plays. How can he be grumpy with gifts like that?*

"We are rather pleased with it. Nathan cut the gingerbread so carefully. We need to have a swing on the front porch, along with a couple of rocking chairs, don't you think?" At her delighted nod, he continued, "We'll make the chain out of wire, perhaps."

"What if we crochet the wire to make the chain—of course, that depends on how fine the wire is."

"What a marvelous idea. You think it possible?"

"I'll have to try. Isn't the wire you hang pictures with made up of finer wires?"

"It is."

Watching the grandfather, she could feel the grandson watching her. When had it grown so stifling in the room? Generally she felt chilly here and so brought a shawl. She carefully folded that across the back of the chair and took up her basket of supplies, setting out the finished things. Henny had woven two rugs on a miniature loom Mr. Hanson had fashioned. Mrs. Hanson had created bedding for the son's room, including two pillows with white slips. Mr. Hanson had carved a trunk with a lid that lifted on tiny hinges of leather and rubbed it with black shoe polish until it shone.

"Those are perfect. What little girl will not be enchanted with all these furnishings?" Lawrence examined the trunk. "What shall we put in it?"

She could feel Nathan behind her. Her heart knew his nearness before he spoke.

"Books, a ball and bat," he said.

The three of them sat down and placed all the furnishings finished so far in place. No room was complete yet, but each had some things in it.

"I'm working on the front door now," Nathan said. "I'll finish that before attaching the porch."

Arley couldn't take her eyes off his fingers as he moved the furniture back out of the parlor. The scar peeked out when he stretched his arm too far. Would he ever tell her what had happened to him? Would asking his grandfather be too nosy?

Again she jerked herself back into ordinary-Arley mode. "I can't stay as long today. Grandmother is insisting that I must accompany her to a tea this afternoon."

Gunderson senior handed Arley a five-inch carving that he was fashioning into a man. "Do you want to make clothes for the dolls also, or should I just carve them on?"

Arley studied the doll. "Carving and painting might be best for now. Our time is getting so short."

"Three days until the party at the orphanage, right?"

"Yes. I checked. They have everything in order."

"Good." Mr. Gunderson nodded.

"And we have to figure out some way to keep the house covered so no one guesses what it is."

"What about that crate in the shed?" Nathan asked.

Mr. Gunderson nodded. "If we put it on its side and use hooks to hold the top in place so we can slide the house out, rather than lift it…" He visually measured the house and headed out the back door. When he returned, he was nodding. "That'll work. Two inches taller and we'd have to build something." He smiled at Arley. "Have you been planning the party, too?"

"Only in the beginning this year. I got them trained so they could handle it."

"No wonder your grandmother prizes you so. You have a good head on your shoulders."

Arley stared at him. Her grandmother didn't prize her; in fact, she rarely had a good word to say, always finding the least little thing wrong. The look on her face must have said more than she wanted it to, when he nodded again. "I know she's headstrong and critical but—"

"How do you know all that?" The words sprang from her lips before she was even aware she'd spoken. "I mean, you've been gone and you never see her now."

"Observation. Listening. From what I hear, she hasn't changed a whole lot through the years, only I think her more negative traits have been winning in recent years. Sometimes that happens when you lose someone you love."

Arley dropped her gaze. This man seemed to see right into one's soul. Did her grandmother really love her husband that much, or was there something else that happened she didn't know about? She thought about asking, but something stopped her. Maybe another time.

When they broke for dinner, she excused herself and headed for home. If she wasn't ready on time, her grandmother would get testy. Not that it mattered exactly when they arrived at the tea. The invitation had said to come between two and four. But Arley had to prepare for the barrage of questions her grandmother was sure to ask. She thought back to the music and the treasured compliment. She'd not even said thank-you. Her manners were indeed appalling.

"If we hurry, we can get that grandfather clock boxed and on the train today. I promised them they'd have it for Christmas."

Nathan nodded and pushed his chair back, picking up the dishes as he stood. "Do you want me to get the wagon?"

"No, I think between us we can carry it."

"It's a ways and slippery."

"We'll put it on the sled, then you can pull me home."

Nathan shook his head, remembering one long-ago winter when he visited and his grandfather had pulled him on a trail through the woods.

"Have you decided yet what you are going to tell your father?" Lawrence asked.

Nathan sighed. "One thing I know, I do not want to

go back to the plant. I want no part of his empire." He paused and looked his grandfather. "Maybe I'll just ignore him and he'll go away."

"More'n likely he'll be down on a train to fetch you, sure that I'm keeping you against your will."

Nathan snorted. "Surely he knows better than that."

"Fear does strange things to a man."

"Fear?" Nathan laid the hammer down on the crate. "My father prides himself on not being afraid of anything."

"He's afraid he's going to lose you, lose all the dreams he has tied up in you. Passing on the legacy of his business to you has always been his dream. That's why he pushed you so hard."

"To fulfill *his* dream. He certainly had no regard for mine."

"That's why it's a shame you had no brothers."

"My sister would do better with the business than I. But he wouldn't countenance a woman in the business realm, so he has two unhappy children. At least Loretta is married and, I think, happy." Which reminded him that he'd not written to his sister much in the past few months, either. Cutting himself off from his former life had not felt like a sacrifice. But when he allowed himself to think about it, he realized his mother had made sure he at least had a *taste* of his dream of music. Enough to give him the skills to aid him in the healing of the past year. Strange how he now considered the accident a blessing beyond measure, while his parents had been sure his life was over.

"We had best hurry or we'll miss the train." Together

they laid the heavy box on the sled and, well bundled up, headed for the train station, Nathan pulling and his grandfather making sure the box didn't fall off.

They could hear the train whistle as they pulled the box up onto the platform via the ramp built for just such a purpose. Lawrence went into the station to pay the freight, leaving Nathan to watch the black monster with one huge eye pull into the station, steam billowing in the cold. The screech of brakes, metal on metal, the clanging bell, all sounds Nathan used to hear ten hours a day at the coal plant. He'd never cared for that sound, while to his father it was as good as counting gold.

A man pushed open the door to a freight car and retrieved the mail sack. Nathan had heard that the town was hoping for a new post office soon, along with a switchboard for the telephones that were also predicted. When his grandfather returned, the two of them hoisted the box up through the freight-car doorway.

"You take good care of that now," Lawrence said to the man. He slapped the box. "Make someone mighty happy this Christmas."

"'Nother of your floor models?"

"*Ja,* one of my best. All that piano wood has come in mighty handy."

The man shook his head and spat a gob of tobacco juice into the snowbank. "We never heard the last of that. Dropping a piano." He shook his head again. "Glad you could use the wood. Been a shame to burn all that."

The whistle blew and Lawrence helped slide the door shut. He turned to Nathan. "Let's stop by and get the mail. Anything we need to home?"

"This one's for you, young man," the clerk said, handing Nathan an envelope.

As soon as he saw the handwriting, he knew. The ax had fallen.

Chapter Eleven

Nathan

"Aren't you going to open it?"

Nathan sat staring at the fire, chin propped on one hand, elbow propped on the chair arm. After long seconds he shook his head. "I know what it says. He never gives up." Staring into the flames brought him no wisdom, no answers. Nathan heaved a sigh. "If I go back to my former life, I will lose all the peace I've gained here."

"You could build a far better wood shop there and work on your violin in your spare time. You don't have to give up the dream."

"There is not enough spare time, working for the company all day, then in the evening either entertaining guests or being a guest elsewhere."

"Have you thought of buying a home of your own? Surely you can say no to some invitations."

"You'd think so, wouldn't you?" His mind slipped into musing. Did he go along with what his father wanted out of duty or devotion, or because it was just far easier to go along than fight about it? And then the accident, and all he could think was to come here, get away from the strictures of society, the rush and the hurry. "I really don't believe I am cut out to be the head of a corporation, the battling and scraping to make the best deals."

"Except in the music world?"

"I'm not sure I'm even competitive enough for that. I think I used to be, but perhaps when my father refused to allow music school, he took that dream away. Perhaps I just gave up." *Or maybe I gave in so easily because I knew somewhere inside that I really wasn't good enough.*

"If you don't go back…"

"What will I do?" Nathan gazed around the room. So unpretentious, so comfortable. So very real. "Are you kicking me out?"

The old man chuckled. "Hardly. Having you here is like having a new life."

"But you seem happy with the life you have."

"Happy? Such a transient thing. Contented, yes. Joyful? Yes. But that comes from inside. You can choose joy and it will be like an artesian well that never runs dry. You can turn it off sometimes, but when you turn it on again, it will gush forth. The Bible promises us that. But if you grab for happiness, it will slip away, like the mist in the morning sun."

"So you're saying I can have joy anywhere if I so choose?"

His grandfather nodded.

"But isn't it easier to find in some places than others?"

"Remember, you are choosing, not finding."

Nathan glanced over at the letter lying on the table in a pool of lamplight.

"'If the Son shall set you free, you will be free indeed,'" Lawrence quoted.

"And that is part of joy?"

"That is the well."

Nathan pushed himself to his feet and fetched his violin case. "Do you mind if I play? I always think better when I do."

"You play and I'll carve. I hope Arley had an enjoyable afternoon with Louise."

Nathan began rosining his bow. "I know there are stories behind the stories regarding Mrs. Dexter. If at any time you feel inclined to share them with me, I'll be glad to listen."

"Play something lively."

It was a good thing her grandmother did not like to overstay her welcome. Arley felt as if her face might crack from all the smiling she'd done. They said their goodbyes, wished everyone a merry Christmas, *God Jule* to those who still spoke Norwegian, and walked out to the sleigh, where Mr. Hanson waited. At their arrival, he took the blankets off the team, and after helping the women get seated, he tucked the wool robes around Arley and her grandmother.

"You didn't stay long."

"Long enough." Louise settled against the cushioned back. "Our leaving gives them plenty of time to gossip about us."

"Grandmother." Arley hid her laughter behind her fur muff.

"I put my donation in an envelope. Mrs. Queen Bee did all but ask me outright what I gave. Now how rude is that?"

"Surely—"

"Surely nothing. That is the only reason she invites me year after year. Polite drivel. And the entertainment? If I couldn't play and sing any better than that, I would certainly not perform."

"She *made* the girls perform—it wasn't their choice." Arley thought of the two young girls, remembering her years of mortification when forced to play the piano before she was accomplished enough. The times she'd been commanded to recite. Sheer agony. But now she *could* play and help guests have a good time, and if called upon, speak in front of a group. She had her grandmother to thank for that.

"Remember all those times you forced me to play or recite or serve tea?"

"Yes, but you were far more accomplished than those two."

"But I was terrified."

"You never showed it. I was proud of your backbone."

Shock at the compliment made Arley turn to stare at her grandmother. "Thank you. You never told me that."

"Of course not. You might have become conceited, and there is nothing more crass than conceit."

"I see." Arley reached over and patted her grandmother's gloved hands. "You have to admit her house was lovely and the food was good."

"That's true and I told her so."

"I'm sure." Arley hoped the tone her grandmother had was genuine and not condescending. Sometimes she wasn't sure if she realized how her so-very-proper words could sound.

"I do hope you are about finished with whatever it is you and the others have been working so hard on."

Arley swallowed. "Ah, you haven't peeked, have you?"

"Peeked? At what?" Attack was sometimes the best way to cover one's guilt.

"Please," she said, "if you have discovered anything, act surprised when the time comes."

"That's all you are going to tell me?"

"Yes."

"Are all the plans in place for the party at the orphanage?"

"As far as I know. I talked with Mrs. Teigen yesterday to see if anything had come up."

"Mrs. Hanson has been baking up a frenzy. You'd think we were providing all the refreshments."

Arley knew she'd made life harder for Cook by not being there to help as she had in the past. But Henny and Mrs. Iverson were assisting, and Mr. Hanson frequently could be found in the kitchen with a towel around his middle and flour on his face.

"Well, two more days and the party will be behind us." Arley gathered her courage since her grandmother seemed in such an agreeable mood. "I've been thinking that we could make life better for some of those children if we brought them to our house for a visit, perhaps one or two at a time. You know, let them have a real bath, perhaps a new dress, and maybe we could start a sewing circle or something."

"Absolutely not!"

The sleigh stopped with a jangle of bells at the front door.

"Thank you, Mr. Hanson," Louise said. "That was a delightful ride." Louise pushed back the robe and stood to get out. Arley leaped out and turned to give her grandmother a hand, then assisted her as they walked up the snow-free but icy walk and steps. Why was she so adamant about not bringing the children to the house? Especially in light of all her sermons on helping others.

"Thank you, my dear," Louise said when they were in the house. "But I have no intentions of falling, and am not so decrepit that you need to hover."

Mrs. Iverson greeted them. "Welcome home. I hope you had a lovely time." She helped Louise out of her coat and hat. "I have tea ready if you would like something to warm you. There's a fire in the library."

"Thank you. Will you join me, Arley?"

What could she say? Resentment hovered. Visions of the towels she was embroidering for the dollhouse tugged at her mind. The thought of the dollhouse brought Nathan to mind, not that he was ever far from it lately. How she yearned to tell her grandmother about the violin music, but if she started, the full story would be out before she knew what hit her.

I might have another surprise for you for Christmas. Could she say that and leave it there? And what if the Gunderson men couldn't come? She'd better extend the invitation first.

"You are mulling over something," Louise said.

"I know, but you can't ask." She poured the tea when Mrs. Iverson brought it in and sat staring into the fire as the two women discussed the afternoon affair. Did her grandmother seem less critical than usual, or was she mistaken?

Nathan stared into the fire after his grandfather climbed the narrow stairs to his bed. Arley. Arlayna. What an unusual name. He still couldn't remember the whole string of names she'd been blessed with, but given time, he was sure he'd learn them. Given time, that was the problem. Time was running out and he'd just begun to realize what a treasure he had found in her, in spite of the fact that she managed to irritate him rather regularly. But when he thought about it, her responses were refreshing. He closed his eyes to see her the better as she'd absorbed the music. She'd not just listened but seemed to take it in through every pore, floating with it, letting the power of it lift and take her away. What kind of man was Handel to write such music?

Dedicated, that was certain. Dedication was an apt word for Miss Dexter, too. And the joy she was having in creating this dollhouse for the children who had nothing! How she managed to get so many people involved, all to surprise her grandmother, who sounded like a bit of a tyrant. Arley and he were just beginning to really talk and now he would have to leave.

He glared at the letter, still unopened. So much more pleasant to think of Arley. Arley, her face framed by the blue felt bonnet. Arley with Eugenia in her lap. Swaying to the music. Arley holding a kitten, such longing on her face. Surely she could have a kitten of her own. Why was that so much to ask?

He blew out a breath, pushed himself to his feet and picked up the letter. His father's handwriting was bold and forceful as always. When he had come to check on his son mid-recuperation, he'd not spent the night, had arrived instead on the morning train and left again on the afternoon. When he and his mother came the first time, Nathan knew she'd been shocked at the size of the cottage, most likely considering this squalor compared to their house in the city or even their house at the lake. The house near Fargo had been much bigger than this.

He picked up a knife and slit the envelope. The urge to toss the whole thing in the fire and forget it had arrived made his hands shake. Instead, he slipped the single sheet of paper out and unfolded it.

Dear Nathan,

You asked me to give you a year and I have complied with your request. It is time that you return to St. Paul and assume your rightful place in the Twin Cities Coal Company. I am grateful that you have fully recovered from your injuries and will always thank my father for being such a large part of that. I will repay him somehow.

Your mother has things well in hand for Christmas and it will be good to have the entire family together for a change. Your sisters have been inquiring after you. It is a shame you have not taken the time to write to them, or us, regularly.

Nathan flinched at the rebuke. What could he say but that it was true? He'd not written often. For a time his hands had shaken so severely from the burn damage that his writing was nearly indecipherable, but thanks to the wood-carving, the tremors had passed.

I look forward to welcoming you home.

Sincerely,
John A. Gunderson.

I want to be *here* for Christmas, Nathan thought. I want to be *here* for the new year and for the days and months after that. I want to pursue a friendship with Arley. I want to finish this violin and start the next one. I want to find the joy my grandfather talks about.

He folded the paper and slid it back in the envelope. Now to figure out how to do it all.

Chapter Twelve

Arley

Those hypocritical old biddies, Arley thought as she threw back the covers. She tried to have a cheerful face by the time she got down to the kitchen, but when she heard Mrs. Hanson whisper, "Uh-oh, Miss Arley is on a rampage," she knew she'd failed somehow.

"If anyone asks for me today, I'll be home when I get done." Already clothed for the frigid out-of-doors, she picked up the basket containing the last of her articles for the dollhouse, along with those the others had finished, and stomped out the door.

Stomping went a long way toward keeping one warm. There was no music flowing from the woodworker's cottage, so she pushed open the door and entered. "Anyone home?"

"Back here." Mr. Gunderson's cheery welcome

helped somewhat, but music might indeed have soothed the savage beast, had Nathan been playing.

Nathan stood at the workbench, working with his violin and glue and clamps. He glanced over his shoulder and nodded to her.

Uh-oh. The grump was back. Well, grump meet grump. She'd already been through her list of shoulds on the way over. She should be cheerful. She should be grateful. She should be accepting of others. She should not be judgmental. She should have and share the spirit of Christmas. This morning she had wanted to throw the shoulds in the creek.

"Good morning." Lawrence stepped back from the dollhouse. "What do you think?"

Arley's jaw dropped. "Oh, it is gorgeous." She walked around the table, staring at the house in total delight. All painted now, gray with navy-and-white trim, the door a deep burgundy. The house even had a tiny Welcome sign by the front door. The swing hung on the porch. All the furniture and furnishings they'd finished were in place.

"You must have stayed up all night." She set her basket on the table and went to remove her outer garments.

"Not quite." Gunderson senior checked on the coffee-pot. "Cold as it is, I thought you might like a warm-up."

"Yes, please." She touched the tiny baby in the cradle with one finger, setting the cradle to rocking. "This is exquisite. I can't wait to see the looks on the girls' faces. And on my grandmother's."

"How did the tea go?" He set the cup and saucer in front of her. "Cream?"

"No, thank you. Today I need it black."

"Something is bothering you." He made a statement, not a question.

"Is it that obvious?" Arley shook her head. "I'm sorry. But yesterday at the tea, they sat around and gossiped and showed off their new gowns. Those women didn't care about the people who needed help. They just cared who donated the most money. And all of them were wearing enough jewelry to feed a poor family for ten years. Yes, they donate, but can't they see there are people who are in desperate need all year around? Are poor people only supposed to get hungry at Christmas?"

Lawrence reached across the table and patted her hand. "You have started something special here and perhaps it will encourage others. I know it has me."

"I have a feeling that the spirit of giving is not something you lack."

"Sometimes we have to go without to learn how rich we really are."

Arley sipped her coffee, so aware of every little sound behind her it was all she could do not to turn and address the younger Gunderson. "Well, I hope you've kept track of all the hours you've worked on this so that I can pay you."

He shook his head. "Oh, no, my dear, this is a work of love on all our parts. There can be no payment."

"I can't thank you enough." Arley's eyes filled with tears. "But you've not given me a bill for repairing the nutcracker or making the new one, though you may not have had time to make the new one, what with the dollhouse."

"I have the bill for the repairing. The new one is not finished yet, but it will be by Christmas."

"You are an amazing man. Grandmother will be so pleased."

Arley sipped her coffee. "I have one more question before I put these things in place. Would the both of you please join us on Christmas Day for dinner and the afternoon?" She leaned forward. "Please say you will come. And you are coming to the party at the orphanage tomorrow, aren't you?"

"Wouldn't miss it. Thank you for the invitations. I would be delighted to come."

She turned to face the workbench. "And you, Nathan, would you be willing to play your violin for us?"

He stopped moving, but for his shoulders, which rose and fell on a deep sigh. Turning, he leaned his hips against the bench. "I'll have to see. Thank you for inviting me."

The pain in his eyes smote her in her midsection. "Are you all right?"

He turned back to the workbench without a word. But later, when they were crating the completed dollhouse, he joined them, but only spoke when asked a direct question and then with as few words as possible.

"I will deliver this in the morning, covered with a canvas," he said.

"Good. I will prepare a bit of a speech and then we can present it." Arley clasped her hands under her chin. "This will be so wonderful."

Halfway home she realized Nathan had not agreed

to come for Christmas, even though his grandfather had. She'd have to ask him again at the party.

Early the next afternoon they loaded up the sleigh with all the baked goods for the party. There was no room in the sleigh now, so Arley and Mrs. Hanson walked over to the orphanage. Three of the girls met them at the door. They pulled Arley into the dining room, where a large wooden box covered by a sheet sat on a table.

"Do you know what it is?" they asked her.

She nodded, trying to hold be a grin, but failed. "But I won't tell so don't even try. It's to be a surprise for tonight."

"Can we ask you questions?"

"If you want, but I won't give any hints away." She led them back to the kitchen to help set up. But every time she walked through the dining room, Nettie was standing in front of the box, staring at it as if by sheer force of will she might see through the coverings. Mrs. Hanson set apple cider to heating and added the spices and sugar. Pink punch filled another bowl, and trays of cookies, breads, cakes and candies were ready to carry in, now covered by dish towels.

When they were finished, Mr. Hanson took Arley home in the sleigh to change into her party frock. Not only would the surprise be wonderful for the children, she'd get to see Nathan again. She finally had Henny help with her hair because it would not behave.

"We're all going to the party." Henny stared at her in the mirror. She leaned close to whisper, "Can't wait to see her face."

Arley knew she meant Grandmother. Perhaps tonight some of what she knew must be a story would come out when her grandmother and Mr. Gunderson met again. The thought gave her goose bumps.

An hour or so later, a buzz of excited people met them as they stepped through the front door of the orphanage. Cedar garlanded the stair railings and hung from the simple chandelier overhead. Arley tucked her grandmother's arm in her own and led the others to the dining room. Garlands festooned the windows and a tree glittered in one corner. But the cloth-covered box had drawn a crowd.

Louise looked at the box, then at her granddaughter. "The surprise?"

"We shall see." Arley glanced around the room, searching for the Gundersons. Surely they wouldn't just not show up. But then she caught a glimpse of Mr. Gunderson coming down the steps and hardly recognized him. He wore a black suit with a gray vest, his hair was trimmed and delight lent sparkle to his eyes.

Her eyes widened and she compressed her lips to keep from laughing out loud. Was this really the man who'd been carving and creating the dollhouse? But he was alone. Her shoulders slumped. Nathan was not coming. She knew it as surely as she saw his grandfather standing there.

"Grandmother, there is someone here I would like you to meet."

"Oh, really? Who?" Louise turned to follow her granddaughter. When she saw Mr. Gunderson, she stopped walking. She caught her breath and straightened, sniffing at the same time. Her jaw tightened, but then…a tear trickled down her cheek.

"Lawrence."

"Hello, Louise. It's been a long time." His eyes never left hers as he held out his hand.

Arley saw her grandmother's hand tremble as she reached for his.

Right at that moment, Mrs. Teigen clapped for order. "Everyone, please find places to sit so we can begin our program." Some of the boys guided people to the chairs lined up in front of the box. Others took seats on the benches that usually lined the tables.

Arley led her group to the front row where the girls had been saving the seats. While it took a while for the assemblage to settle down, Louise never let go of Arley's hand. Mr. Gunderson sat next to her. Curiosity ran rings around Arley's mind, but she could do nothing at the moment.

Louise leaned close to whisper in Arley's ear. "How did…?"

Arley shook her head and whispered back, "Later."

A small group of children sang a medley of songs. Arley wished Nathan had been there with his violin to accompany them. Several recited pieces, and Mrs. Teigen gave out awards for good grades and good behavior. The children handed out cards they had made to thank the people who supported the orphanage. All the girls wore the new hair ribbons Arley had given them.

Soon Arley would present the special gift. She had butterflies on her butterflies. Would her grandmother appreciate the dollhouse? Had she let her own dreams get away with her? She knew the children would be entranced. *Please, Lord, help me say just the right things.* She glanced around her grandmother and got a smile from Lawrence that made her feel all would be well.

Mrs. Teigen took her place in the front again. "Now I would like to turn the program over to Miss Arley Dexter, who has a special surprise for us all."

Arley squeezed her grandmother's hand and, after taking a deep breath, stood and turned to the gathered people. "Good evening and thank you all for coming. Thank you for supporting this orphanage and the children who live here."

Nettie gazed up at her from the group of girls sitting cross-legged in front of the chairs. Her smile gleamed like sunbeams.

Arley had to pause a moment to get her thoughts in order. "I was trying to think of what to give my grandmother for Christmas this year when a little girl here gave me an idea." She smiled down at Nettie. "So I went home and thought about it and decided to ask a friend of mine if he would help me make this surprise. Since it was so close to Christmas, I asked others if they would help, too." She listed the names of her grandmother's staff. "Would you all and Mr. Lawrence Gunderson please stand?" As they did, she began applauding and so did the others. The collective anticipation in the room was almost palpable. "Our creation is being given to the Willow Creek Orphanage in honor of my grandmother, Mrs. Louise Dexter. Merry Christmas, Grandmother." She beckoned to Mr. Hanson and

Mr. Gunderson to help her. They removed the cloth to reveal the packing crate. Mr. Gunderson unlatched one side and Mr. Hanson the other.

No one even breathed as they waited.

Slowly the front of the crate was lowered. "Oooh," the girls in front gasped.

The gasp of delight made Arley's eyes leak.

The men withdrew the dollhouse and the sounds of wonder spread through the entire audience. Several of the older boys removed the crate completely and the men set the dollhouse on the table. One of the girls started to clap and within moments everyone was clapping. Arley looked at her grandmother. She had tears streaming down her face and wasn't even trying to wipe them away. Arley nodded to the two men and they turned the table around so that everyone could see inside the house. The applause increased. Nettie leaped to her feet and threw herself into Arley's arms.

Looking up, she beamed. "You made the story come true, you did."

Arley hugged her, then addressed the entire assemblage. "Thank you all for coming. Now, while the girls explore their treasure, refreshments will be served on the other side of the room. I just want to remind you of the box by the tree where you are welcome to drop your donations. The children will have presents to open on Christmas morning, thanks to your generosity."

As the guests rose, Arley knelt in front of her grandmother. "This is what took all of our time."

Louise cupped Arley's face in her hands. "What a perfect present! When I was a little girl, I wanted a dollhouse but there was no money for such foolishness. I know you wanted one at one time, too, and now we all have one. Thank you." She leaned close to whisper, "I would have loved to help make this."

"Sorry, but I wanted so badly to surprise you."

"You did. You did indeed."

When her grandmother stood, Lawrence was right by her side. Together they joined the gaggle of girls admiring each room and each piece of furnishing.

If only Nathan were here, Arley thought as she accepted the congratulations from the guests. What had kept him away?

Chapter Thirteen

Christmas Day

How was it possible to be so happy and so sad at the same time?

Arley pondered that question as she dressed on Christmas morning. She was happy for her grandmother, whom she'd even caught singing in the sewing room! Since Lawrence Gunderson had strolled back into her life, she'd invited him for supper twice and seconded Arley's invitation for Christmas Day. He'd accompanied them to the Christmas Eve service the night before and, much as she suspected, had a thrilling singing voice.

Arley had spent part of the past two days practicing at the piano so she wouldn't make a fool of herself when guests came and singing carols was part of the entertainment. Her fingers remembered the notes better than she'd thought they would, and she'd enjoyed filling the house with music.

If only… And that was where the sad part came in. If only Nathan had not turned his back on Willow Creek and gone to St. Paul instead. Thoughts of why he'd left had ravaged her sleep. Why did he not give her a message? Why would Mr. Gunderson not tell her why his grandson had left? He said only that it was a family matter. Yet when she'd asked if he was coming back, he said he didn't know, but that he hoped so.

Was hope enough to get her through a day that should be one of the most joyful of the year?

But possibly she'd only imagined the thrill when she'd touched his hand. He had led such a different life from hers, perhaps he…

She was tired, discouraged and sad. She'd even awakened crying during the night. During the day she kept an iron clamp on her feelings so that no tears dared chase others down her cheeks.

She jerked the snood off her hair. Not even her hair would behave. Attacking her flying tresses with the hairbrush, she glared at her face in the mirror. "You will be happy today if it kills you! Do you understand me?"

"Please, miss…"

Arley looked up to see Henny standing nervously in the doorway. She laid the hairbrush on the dressing table. "I'm sorry, Henny. What is it?"

"C-can I help you with your hair?"

"I would be delighted if you would."

"Why didn't you call me?"

"I should at least be able to control my own hair, don't you think?" Since she couldn't seem to control this other thing that had her trapped in its clutches. She didn't know what to call it other than disappointed. Caring would have to do. The feeling started out with meeting a grumpy man and ended with the grumpy man leaving. Without a word. Oh, but the beauty and the glory of the time in between. Listening to him play, watching him work so painstakingly on the violin and the dollhouse. Hearing his voice, that rich baritone that closely resembled his grandfather's. If only there had been time for the growing friendship to blossom into something more.

Henny quickly twisted and wrapped and pinned, then laid her hands on Arley's shoulders. "There you go, Miss Arley. You look lovely today."

With dark circles under her eyes and no joy in them? How could Henny say that? "Thank you. You are a wonder when it comes to fixing hair."

"Breakfast is ready whenever you come downstairs."

"Is Grandmother already down?"

"Yes, but she said there was no hurry."

"My grandmother said that?" Arley's eyebrows tickled the bangs she'd snipped two days earlier. She smiled into the mirror, reflecting Henny's delighted gaze.

Henny nodded. "*Your* grandmother."

The two of them headed downstairs to the one meal a year that everyone in the house ate together, a tradition Arley insisted on two years earlier, the first time she had really stood up to her grandmother as an adult. She walked into the dining room to discover a guest there, Lawrence Gunderson, not dressed as nattily as he had been at the party, but still in fine wool slacks, a long-sleeved shirt and a sweater. Surely there was more to this man than she had presumed.

"Good morning." At least his voice was still the same. "Merry Christmas."

"Merry Christmas to you." Her voice wasn't wobbling, was it? But when she looked at her grandmother, all she saw were smiles.

"Lawrence, if you would sit there." Louise motioned to her right and then Arley to her left. The rest of the staff filled in the chairs and Mrs. Hanson brought in platters of ham, potatoes and scrambled eggs to join the *lefse* and *Julekake*, sliced so the candied bits of fruit showed, applesauce pinked with cinnamon candies, and muffins. When Mrs. Hanson took her place, they all bowed for the Norwegian grace that was kept special for the holidays. When finished, they passed the platters around, conversation picking up as if they were all old friends, instead of family and the helpers.

Lawrence commented on the nutcracker collection, winking at Arley when Louise was looking the other way. He'd brought the new one with him the day before when he came to take her grandmother for a sleigh ride. So there was another package under the tree with her name on it.

When they'd finished eating and were enjoying coffee refills, Louise tapped her glass with her knife. When the room grew quiet, she sat slightly forward. "I know you all have a horde of questions, so I will tell you all at once. Lawrence and I grew up near here and went to the same school. We knew we were in love, but when my father decided I was of marrying age, he insisted that I marry Mr. Dexter, and when Lawrence learned that, he disappeared. I did as my father ordered and Mr. Dexter and I had many happy and prosperous years together and one son. When Arlayna came to live with me after the train wreck that killed our son and her mother, we reared her as our own. When Dexter died, I continued with his business interests, and as you all know, we have fared very well. Until Lawrence walked into the orphanage two days ago, I did not know if he would ever speak to me again. While I'd heard he had moved back here, I was afraid to contact him. All those years." She shook her head. "But he helped you all in the creation of that magnificent dollhouse, and I will be ever grateful that he has come back into my life. Thank you, Arlayna, for the part you played in this…this comedy of errors?" She smiled at Arley, who shrugged. It wasn't a tragedy, that was for sure. "And thank you all for your work on the dollhouse and giving it in my name. There was even a small plaque with my name on it on the side of the house. I am indeed honored and privileged to have all of you working for and with me." She raised her coffee cup. "Merry Christmas to us all." She pushed back her chair. "And now let us open our presents."

She led the way into the parlor where the tree stood in front of the window, candles ready to be lit. When everyone was seated, she motioned Arley to hand around the gifts.

Arley handed the package to her grandmother first. "From me."

"But you…" Louise took the package and shook it

gently. "Long, narrow. Is this what I'm thinking it might be?"

"You'll have to open it to find out."

Everyone watched as Louise opened the box and lifted out a hand-carved nutcracker. It stood at attention, the arm that was saluting the mechanism to work the jaw to crack the nuts. But instead of a soldier's hat, he wore a black derby, and a gold-painted watch fob closed his red vest. Long pants, instead of lederhosen, and dress shoes, instead of boots, a contemporary gentleman. She held him up, her face wreathed in smiles. "And I know who made him." She turned the figure upside down to show the initials LG and 1910 on the flat surface. "Thank you, Arley. I'm sure you had no idea that I had another with those initials from long ago."

Arley blushed crimson. "I *did* know, Grandmother. It was the one I fell on and broke, then had repaired by Mr. Gunderson. Someone told me a wood-carver had set up shop on the little road north of town, and I went to him to see if he could repair it."

"And I did," Lawrence said. "And look what the Lord has caused to happen." He spread his arms wide. He reached behind his chair and pulled out a box with holes in the sides. "This is for you, Arley."

A mew came from inside the box as Arley lifted off the lid. The gray kitten with white feet looked up at her. Her gaze flew to her grandmother, who nodded with not quite a smile. "He really is mine?" Arley asked.

"He needs to go back to his mother for a few more weeks, but he really is yours."

Arley sat down with the kitten in her lap, stroking his head and back.

"So, the rest of the gifts?" Louise whispered.

"Oh, sorry," Arley said with a smile.

"I'll pass them out," Henny said. "You hold your kitten and think of a name for him."

Sometime later, when the wrappings were all folded and put in a box, the packets of gift money given out and the staff had cleared off the table and were in the kitchen preparing dinner, Arley turned from the kitten dozing on her lap and looked up to see Mr. Gunderson watching her.

"Thank you," she said, "if I forgot to say it before."

"You are welcome indeed. I had to do a bit of arm-twisting to get your grandmother to agree, but she really is soft at heart."

Arley didn't bother to argue with him, although those had never been words she would have used to describe her grandmother. He'd probably been away too long to know the real Louise. But if the look of peace on her grandmother's face was any indication, perhaps God had indeed worked a Christmas miracle.

The doorbell had begun to ring as guests began arriving for dinner and the afternoon's festivities. As usual, Arley acted as hostess, taking people's coats and pointing them in the direction of the parlor, where some were gathering, and the sunroom, where others were.

The bell chimed again and she answered a question over her shoulder as she opened it. "Please come—" Her voice froze. Nathan Gunderson stood on the steps, violin case under one arm and a carpet bag beside him.

"You came back," she said.

"I was to be here earlier, but the train was late."

She stared into his eyes, no longer seeing the hurt and anger there, but a steady gaze that warmed her clear to her toes. "I…ah…won't you, I mean…" She took a step back. "Please come in." Surely he could hear her heart pounding.

"You invited me to play, remember?"

"But you never answered me."

"I knew I had to go talk with my father, and I wasn't sure how it would go."

"I see," she said, not seeing anything at all but the upward curve of his lips. He was truly smiling.

"You missed the party." She held out her arms for his cloak.

"But I am here for this one." He hung his hat on the hall tree. Then he leaned closer and lowered his voice. "And my grandfather and your grandmother, are they, I mean, is everything all right?"

She resisted the urge to touch his cheek. "They are like two magnets you cannot pull apart."

"So there is romance in the air?"

"We shall see." She led the way into the parlor where her grandmother was holding court. "Grandmother, I want you to meet Mr. Nathan Gunderson, the other Gunderson who worked so deftly on the dollhouse. Mr. Gunderson, my grandmother, Mrs. Dexter."

"Well, young man, I was beginning to have my doubts that you would make it."

"Had the train gone any slower, I would have gotten out and walked." He bowed slightly over her hand.

"Welcome and Merry Christmas." She glanced at Arley and said quietly, "He did bring his violin, didn't he?"

"Yes, he did."

"Good."

Arley wished it could have been the one he made, but she knew that would take many coats of lacquer and hours of sanding before it would be ready to play. She'd read up on violin making in the encyclopedia in the library.

"Have you had anything to eat?" When he shook his head, Louise continued, "There are appetizers in the other room to tide you over until dinner, which will be served in about an hour."

The doorbell rang again and Arley turned to answer it, but saw Henny hurrying down the hall in her place. So instead, she showed Nathan the way to the food table.

"Is my grandfather not here?"

"He took Gabriel back to the comfort of his family."

"Gabriel?"

"My kitten."

"I see. I thought your grandmother…"

"There have been many changes here in the past few days. Would you like hot cider, eggnog or coffee to drink?" Her fingers kept wanting to reach out and touch him, make sure he was real, but her mind was adamant. She would behave in a proper manner.

The only remaining seat was the piano bench, so she sat him there and joined him when he patted the space beside him.

"Do you play?"

She nodded. "Adequately."

"We could play together?" His eyes spoke more eloquently than his words. Was she reading his language correctly? How could she know, for she'd never done this before. Only what she'd read in novels, but if this was drowning in his eyes, she'd better come up for air.

"Arley, is it possible that you could care for a man who has terrible moods at times?"

She gasped as his words struck her heart. She gathered her courage. "Is it possible that you could care for an outspoken woman?"

"Indeed, yes. You are a part of the reason I told my father I was not coming back to work in the family business, and while he is not happy with that, I most certainly am."

"So what are you going to do?"

"Make violins, work for my grandfather. I will no longer be wealthy, but I have enough to live comfortably." He gazed into her eyes again, this time touching the back of her hand with the tips of his fingers. "Shall I ask your grandmother if I may court you?"

"I think that would be a very good idea."

"Perhaps we should build another dollhouse. So that I can see you every day."

She smiled back at him, turning her hand over so he could stroke her palm. The shivers running up her arm made her neck warm and then her cheeks. If this was indeed turning into love as she suspected, surely this was another Christmas miracle, a second for the house of Dexter. Nathan had come back, the finest gift for the finest Christmas.

* * * * *

DISCUSSION QUESTIONS

1. Although Arley and Louise are both strong-willed women, who have each suffered loss and sorrow, they live their lives from different perspectives. What characteristics contribute to Arley's compassion and Louise's disdain?

2. Do you think Arley was right to hide the dollhouse gift from her grandmother since it would be a public presentation rather than private? What was she hiding herself from?

3. Nathan found healing through his music. What other areas of creativity in *The Finest Gift* contribute to healing? Which do you most identify with or wish you could do? Why?

4. Nathan seemed to think there were only two opposite ways to settle the conflict with his father. What other ways could there be?

5. Orphanages and other public institutions have undergone extensive changes since the early 1900s. Do you think the attitudes displayed in the story toward caring for the needy have changed, also, or are still just as mixed? What underlying premise determines choice?

Prologue

Montana Territory, December 7, 1883

Another job done, Rafe Jones thought with satisfaction as he tucked the bounty money he'd collected into his billfold. The bitter-cold streets of Helena were nearly deserted this time of evening. While he stood in darkness, lamplight shone from upstairs apartment windows and neat rows of houses.

Hard to imagine what life might be like inside those homes. He took a moment to ponder it. The faint sound of jingle bells from the next street broke the oppressive quiet. It was nearly Christmas, and tonight most folks were with family and glad to be there. Rafe shook his head. He couldn't imagine it. The only memories he had of family were best forgotten.

He was just reaching to untie his gelding's reins from the hitching post when he heard nearly silent footsteps on the frozen earth behind him. Trouble? It was hard to tell. There was no punch of warning in his gut. No rise of the hair at the back of his neck. He drew his gun, anyway. Better to be safe than sorry.

But when he spun around on his boot heel, the street was bare, the night still. No one lurked in the dark. He scanned the hard-to-see place on the near side of the boardwalk. Huh. He was sure he'd sensed something. He could feel something—

The edge of his jacket was tugged sharply. At the same time he heard a small intake of breath. He looked down and saw the top of a child's head, which had been blocked from sight by his drawn weapon. So, he wasn't alone.

"M-mister?"

He holstered his Colt and took a good look at the kid. A little girl with sleek fine hair shining platinum in the faint lamplight glow. Maybe ten years old. Hard for him to tell, since he wasn't around kids much, not in his line of work. She looked bedraggled, even in the shadows, in a ragged wool coat a few sizes too big for her with half the buttons missing. The skirt of her dress, visible beneath the coat hem, had more patches than original calico.

Poor thing. "You lost your ma?"

"How did you know?" Her round eyes stared up at him in wonder. Pretty, light-colored eyes, which were too big for her heart-shaped face. "My name's Holly and I heard you talkin' to the sheriff when I was sweeping the boardwalk for the missus."

Had a child been outside sweeping when he'd arrived with his latest quarry? He hadn't been paying any mind.

He'd had business to tend to. "You'd best go home, little girl. It's mighty cold out here. Feels like it's fixin' to snow."

"That's why you gotta help me, mister. I wanna go h-home." Her voice broke over that last word.

Hard not to feel touched by that. He drew himself up straight, determined to do his best not to be. "The sheriff's still in his office. You'd best go ask him to take you home."

"He can't help me none. I already asked." There were no tears, only stark sadness in those big eyes. "I heard the missus saying that you was the kind of man who found people who run off. Maybe you could find my ma."

"No." The word was out of his mouth before he could even think it. "Sorry, kid. I don't track missing parents. Likely as not, she took off for a reason. You don't want a ma like that, anyway. I know from personal experience."

"But, mister, I been praying and praying for the angels to help me. I started when Pa first took sick and I didn't stop, not when he died. Not even when I had to go to the home or when I got hired out to work for Missus Beams." There was nothing but pain on her little face and honest innocence in her voice. "The angels musta heard me cuz they sent you."

A tight feeling hit him dead center. The next thing he felt was the punch of alarm in his gut and the quiver of the hair on the back of his neck.

Yep, he was in a whole mess of trouble. The warning had come too late.

Chapter One

Angel Falls, December 16

He was a poor excuse for a bounty hunter, yessir. Rafe flipped an extra nickel onto the scarred wooden bar, ignored the grit and cigar smoke thick in the roadhouse's air and did his best not to think about what buying this sarsaparilla would do to his hard-won reputation.

"No whiskey?" the barkeep grumbled around his plug of tobacco.

"I'll let you know when my tongue needs wettin'." He wasn't keen on liquor. It had been the downfall of his pa. He might not have much schoolin', but he was at least smart enough to learn from his pa's mistakes.

He grabbed the glass and didn't let the looks from the men at the bar bother him none. Then again, if having a little girl at his heels hadn't damaged his reputation as the toughest gun in three Western territories, then a sarsaparilla wouldn't have much effect.

With her chin on her hands, Holly stared gloomily at a knot in the tabletop. Trouble, that was what he felt as he wove between the tables. He'd forked over cash to that horrible Mrs. Beams for the child, no questions asked, and ever since his responsibility for the orphan girl weighed on him.

Lucky break that he was immune to soft feelings of any kind. He was especially immune to big blue eyes as pure as the great Montana sky and blond curls that framed a porcelain face. Even in orphanage castoffs, poorly fitted and so worn that the patches were patched, she didn't tug at his feelings. Not a bit.

"Thank you, Mr. Rafe." She sure looked happy. A treat like this she would never have had in any orphanage or working for that Beams woman. "My pa got me a sarsaparilla once a long time ago. I don't hardly remember it."

He slid the drink onto the table in front of her and took his seat, kept a good watch on the men around him and put his back to the wall. The little girl gripped the glass with both hands and took a dainty sip.

Rafe looked away. He couldn't let in a single feeling. No good ever came from that. He thought of the fancy sewing kit made of pearl and gold that belonged to Holly's ma. He was helping her in hopes of a finder's fee, not because of big eyes that had more worry and vulnerability in them than he knew what to do with. Really.

"I like it," she said simply with a small smile. "It reminds me of my pa."

Yep, he had his heart set against her. The last thing

he intended to do was get attached. He eased the chair back a ways from the table to give himself more space.

"So, are we gonna find my ma now?" She studied him over the top of her glass as she sipped more of the drink.

"*We* aren't gonna do anything." How many times had he told her that? "You'll be staying at the hotel with the woman I'm payin' to watch you. I don't want to hear another word about it."

He scowled, not enough to scare her, but so she'd know not to start askin' him a thousand questions. Again. He'd never come across a more talkative being. Conversing with her, why, it was the first step toward getting hooked. He was a loner and liked it that way.

While the girl sipped—why didn't she just gulp it down and be done with it?—he considered their surroundings. The roadhouse wasn't much better than a saloon. Not a good place for a child, but it wasn't as if he was welcome in the finer establishments in town. He knew that from personal experience, too.

There were a few rough folk he intended to keep a close eye on. That gunslinger at the bar, for example. He looked like trouble. The man was lean and restless, wearing patched-up boots, homemade trousers and a tailored woolen jacket far too fine for the rest of his clothing.

Stolen, no doubt. The polished, expensive Colt Peacemaker holstered at his hip, tied down securely to his belt and thigh with the safety snap free, said it all. That one was lookin' for trouble. Men with that attitude tended to find it. Rafe kept his eye on him, even when the cook brought them their food.

The girl eyed the roast-beef sandwich and stew hungrily. The long ride over the mountain pass had been hard on her, and he regretted that. But since he had a whole Continental Divide of regrets, he could only knuckle back his hat and brace himself for what was coming next.

She folded her hands together, bowed her head and peered at him through her lashes with a schoolmarm look, waiting for him to do the same. He obliged, although it had been a long time since he'd believed enough to bow his head.

"Dear God, please bless this food," she began in her high-noted voice. "And bless Mr. Rafe for takin' me to find my ma. Please let her be prayin' to see me, too. Amen."

His gut twisted up. He grabbed his sandwich and took a bite. "Remember what I told you?"

"Not to get the cart in front of the horse?"

"Yep. Or your high hopes might be in for a hard fall." He couldn't seem to find the words to say what else he was afraid of. How disappointment would drive the innocence out of her like a mean winter wind. In his work, he didn't see the good side of life—or of people. He cleared his throat, which had started to ache. "You can start hopin' when I tell you to."

"Yes, Mr. Rafe." She sipped of her sarsaparilla, looking as if she didn't believe him one bit.

The rough at the bar eyed him with challenge. There was no mistaking it. Not in the mood, Rafe met his gaze and gave a growl. Seconds beat by before the trouble-maker turned away. Backed down. Good.

The girl had gone right on talking. "Do ya think we can find my ma before Christmas? Do you think she's nice? She's gotta be nice."

"There's no telling what kind of woman she might be." He wasn't a gambling man, but if he was, he'd bet Miss Cora Sims might not be the pure and loving mama Holly made her out to be.

And if that reminded him of a boy he'd once known, staring at the rafters trying to fall asleep while listening to the other orphan boys slumbering or crying in their beds, then he wasn't about to admit it. Nope, not at all. Life's road had changed him into a hard man. That boy he'd been was as good as dead. Worse, it was as if that boy had never existed at all.

"You eat up. I've got a lot to do before nightfall."

He could feel that itch at the back of his neck and the chill in his bones. A storm would hit before long— it was only a bad storm and not trouble. He slid his gaze toward the bar.

The troublemaker—and his polished Peacemaker— was gone.

Cora Sims felt the oddest sensation, standing alone behind the counter of her dress shop. The front door was closed and locked, her business done for the day. She felt watched, and she couldn't say precisely why. The dark boardwalks teemed with folks hurrying about their last business of the day—she could see them past the image of the store reflected in the front windows—and no one stood on her step to be let in for a last-minute purchase.

Perhaps this was all the aftereffects of a long day. She tucked the last of her deposit money into her reticule. There. She would stop by the bank on her way home. She didn't have anyone waiting for her these days. She'd taken in her nephews years ago, but they were young men out on their own now. Her cozy house on the edge of town felt empty without them. Thinking of her vacant home, she found her feet dragging a bit as she extinguished the last lamp by the door and let herself out into the cold December air.

"Evening, Miss Sims!" Rhett Jorgenson called out from a few storefronts down, where he was sweeping his stretch of boardwalk. He looked dashing in his fur coat and cap. "I noticed your shop was busier than mine today."

"Yes, it was, thank the Lord. Have a good evening." She waggled her fingers in a wave as she locked her door and headed out, leaving the handsome shoemaker without a backward glance.

Oh, she'd long stopped hoping that the man would take more than polite notice of her. And if her heart painfully squeezed a bit, she no longer noticed such things. She was officially a spinster now, today, her thirtieth birthday. How had she gotten so old so fast?

Another male voice called out, "Evening, Miss Sims."

It was Mr. Dorian, the land-office agent, middle-aged and happily married, who had always been a good neighbor to her. "Good evening, Abe. I set aside a velvet-encased sewing kit. I noticed your wife admiring it when she was in last week."

"Did she now?"

"No obligation." She stopped by his front door. "I will tuck it out of sight just in case you want to consider it. Tell Maryanne hello for me."

"Will do." He checked his lock. "You be careful walking alone. It's dark this time of year and there are plenty of strangers in town."

Cora mentally rolled her eyes. She was quite used to the men of this town treating her like an old spinster in need of advice. She thanked Mr. Dorian politely and continued on to the end of the block. In her sensible brown wool coat, hat and shoes, she knew what everyone in this town saw—a plain woman beyond her prime.

The trouble was, she was starting to feel that way about herself. She caught her reflection in the hardware-store window. A woman too tall and too slim to be considered fashionable stared back at her. It was a blessing she couldn't see the tiny lines on her face. Not wanting to think about *those,* she crossed the street and kept walking.

The jangle of a hand bell broke through her thoughts. Reverend Hadly stood on the street corner with a collection tin on a stand in front of him. "Evening, Miss Sims," he said. "You wouldn't be able to spare a few pennies for the orphan fund, would you?"

"You already know the answer to that." She opened her reticule and extricated a coin from beneath the thick deposit envelope. She dropped the five-dollar gold piece into the tin. Before her minister could comment, she explained, "Business has been very good for me this year. I might as well share a bit of it with those less fortunate."

"Bless you, Miss Sims." The minister smiled broadly. "I'll see you on Sunday."

She nodded once in agreement and hurried on. There was that odd sensation again, the feeling she was being watched. She glanced behind her, but everyone was busily scurrying from one errand to another. The thickening darkness made it hard to see very far. Perhaps her imagination was playing tricks on her. The rigorous day was catching up to her, no doubt. Good thing she was on her way home.

Ahead of her, the horse-and-wagon traffic had come to a halt. She was nearing the heart of the small town, the center of commerce. The boardwalk up ahead looked jammed. The *toot-toot* of the departing train on the far side of town alerted her to the time. She had five minutes to make it to the bank. The last thing she wanted to do was carry this much money home overnight, so she ducked down the side street, intending to cut through the alley. Her thoughts returned to the evening ahead.

She'd not heard from her nephews all day long. It seemed as if she would spend her birthday evening alone. Oh, she couldn't blame the boys for forgetting her. They were so busy these days. The oldest, Emmett, was teaming full-time, and making a good name for himself in the business. And younger Eli was working on a ranch a mile from town—

A shadow separated itself from the darkness and cut into her thoughts. She saw a broad-brimmed hat and a lanky shoulder. She blinked, trying to bring the man into better focus. One of the shopkeepers, perhaps, taking out his garbage? Then why did a hot, prickly urge to run skid through her veins?

The steely click of a revolver's hammer echoed against the unlit backs of the buildings and into the chambers of her heart. A man with a gun. Here, in peaceful Angel Falls? Fear snaked through her and she stumbled back, glancing over her shoulder. But the lit street behind her seemed impossibly far away.

"Don't run," a stranger's voice barked as he stormed closer, his boots harsh on the hard-packed earth, his gun pointed at her. "Don't you do it."

She froze. Nothing but a wheeze of air passed over her tongue. Words failed her utterly. A bubble of panic popped in her chest. She realized the man with the gun was talking, but she couldn't make out his words. Her pulse roared in her ears. He wrenched her reticule from her. The string around her wrist burned as it tore across her hand and came free. She stared directly at the nose of the gun. Was he going to shoot her?

"You tell the sheriff, and I'll hunt you down. Got it?" The robber moved back a few steps, his gun still aimed at her. "I'll know if you do."

She opened her mouth, but no sound came out. He was already gone, running through the darkness. His footsteps echoed in the narrow alley like strikes of a hammer on a nail.

She was shaking, but it wasn't from the bitter December cold. She waited until the sound died away, until the man blurred around the lamp-lit corner and disappeared from her sight. His threat echoed in her head. *You tell the sheriff, and I'll hunt you down.* She didn't doubt it at all.

Now what did she do? She covered her face with her hands. She was fine. She was unharmed. It was only money that he'd taken. Thank the Lord. Delayed fear began kicking through her in rapid jerks. Her knees trembled, and as she took a step, they turned watery. Her hand shot out to grab the mercantile wall for support. There was a rushing sound in her ears. Her heart beat thickly and painfully.

If only she could make it the dozen or so steps out onto the street, she would be even more thankful. Her feet had gone numb. Her ribs felt as if an iron band squeezed them, but she was able to breathe in the fresh cold air. It cleared her head and chased the fear from her blood. Feeling better, she stumbled onto the busy boardwalk.

Was the gunman watching her now from some safe vantage point? She glanced around at the riders on horseback and sitting on wagon seats, at the men loading up wagons and carrying packages for their wives. The gunman's threat wasn't the only reason she couldn't report this. Even thinking of the new sheriff made her stomach seize up. She did not like that man. Perhaps it would be better just to keep silent about what happened. It hardly mattered, now that the money was gone.

Yes, she thought with relief. That was exactly what she would do.

The clock tower in the town square tolled the hour.

Six o'clock. She stood on the boardwalk, not at all sure what to do. The bank vice president, Mr. Wessox, stood in front of the double doors, locking them. She stood empty-handed, feeling the beat of the cold wind.

"Excuse me."

Cora blinked, looking up. She was blocking the middle of the walkway. Why hadn't she realized that sooner? A young mother with a baby in a carriage was unable to pass. The baby was just a wee thing, bundled up in flannel and wool. Cora apologized, stepping back until the wood siding of the mercantile bit her spine.

"Aunt Cora!" A bright baritone rose above the thud of boots hurrying toward her on the boardwalk. "There you are! When you weren't at the shop, I tried the bank, but you weren't there, either. I'm glad I found you, or Emmett would have my hide."

"Eli." All it took was one look at her young nephew's wide grin and handsome face—at eighteen there was still a bit of boy left in him—and fondness filled her. She'd always had a soft spot for this one. Goodness, had he gotten even taller since she'd last seen him two days ago? When he reached her, the shock and fear from the robbery rolled off her like water off a tin roof.

Money didn't matter. Being here for the boys did. "What are you doing here, young man? Oughtn't you be at your job?"

"Mr. Worthington let me go early when I told him about our special plans." He offered her his arm. "What? Do you think we would forget your birthday?"

Gratitude pierced her heart like a blade. She hurt with the sweetness of it. She hurt with the knowledge that soon Emmett and Eli would have wives and families of their own, which was good for them, but she would be achingly alone again.

Determined to enjoy this moment, she slipped her arm in the crook of Eli's strong one. "What do you have planned? I hope you didn't go to any trouble on my account."

"Not a lick of trouble, promise." The breadth of his easy grin said otherwise as they started down the boardwalk together.

Directly in front of the law office, she felt that odd sensation. It was not a friendly feeling. Strange, wasn't it, how she'd felt this way twice before she was robbed? What if the thief was back? What if he tried to steal from her nephew, too?

She turned slowly, the frost on the boardwalk crunching beneath her heels. As a bitter gust of wind assailed her, she saw him. Not the man who'd robbed her, but a man even more intimidating. She froze, overwhelmed by his image, bringing her nephew to a stop alongside her.

"What is it, Aunt Cora?" Eli glanced around. "Is it Emmett? Do you see him? He's supposed to be waiting for us at the hotel."

The boy's words stayed in the background of her mind. The details of the busy street, the festive strings of holly and cranberries, of garlands and fir boughs decorating the shops, the clatter of the traffic on the street and the sting of the first flakes of snowfall faded into nothingness. She was aware only of the man and his gazing at her intensely as if he knew her well, as if he could see her every secret. He was dressed all in black. He was broad-shouldered and tall, his boot-clad feet braced and planted on the boardwalk. A Stetson hat shaded his brow, and even if it had been high noon, that granite face of his would still have been shadowed. A revolver sat holstered on either hip.

Definitely dangerous. Definitely trouble. Cora gulped, realizing he'd spurred himself into motion and was striding purposefully toward her like a mountain lion stalking its prey, a big man who seemed bad as they came. Only then did she notice her reticule clutched in one of his big, rough hands.

Chapter Two

Rafe strode closer, ignoring all but Cora Sims. It had taken him all but a week to find her. He had a sense for things, a natural talent for tracking. It had been the one gift the Lord had seen fit to give him. Now his job was to figure out what kind of woman she was. His natural sense told him not to underestimate the prim, proper-looking woman on the arm of a boy who was maybe eighteen, give or take. Her son? He wished Holly had been able to tell him more about her missing mother.

He eyed Cora Sims from the top of her brown bonnet to the polished tips of her brown shoes. He'd been keeping a close eye on her, sizing her up from a distance. As he thrust out the reticule, he could see things he'd not been able to see from across the street or through the sun-glazed windows of her shop.

She was pretty. One had to be close enough to see it because her beauty was not a loud or brash beauty. No, hers was subtle and quiet as if she were made of pure kindness. Not the sort of woman who easily abandoned a child, he'd wager, and judging by the shining goodness of the young man at her side, she was a fine mother, too.

There was that warning again, a leaden lump in his gut. Something was wrong; something wasn't as it seemed.

"My reticule." She smiled up at him, allowing the lamplight from the mercantile window to spill beneath the brim of her hat and onto her face. "How did you know…?"

"That it was yours? Well, ma'am, I saw what happened. I was standing near the bank and happened to catch sight of you in the alley." Not the whole truth, because he hadn't happened to see her; he'd been purposefully observing her. "I caught that piece of garbage by the scruff of his neck and dropped him off at the sheriff's office."

"You caught him?" Her eyes were luminous—the lamplight revealed light blue eyes deep with feeling. It was as if her entire heart shone there. "But, sir, that man was armed."

"Guns don't worry me much." He jammed his fists in his jacket pockets, unaffected by her. "I only did the right thing."

"Oh, if only everyone would do the same, then what a better world this would be."

"I can't argue with you there, ma'am." He shifted his weight. She was a dainty thing, fine-boned and willowy, and she made him feel every inch of his six feet, two inches. He'd never felt so big and awkward and rough. Why was that bothering him? He was used to being an outsider, used to being viewed as dangerous and unacceptable.

The trouble was, Miss Cora Sims wasn't looking at him that way. No, not at all. A gentle smile tugged at the corners of her mouth. Snowflakes clung to the soft curls peeking out from beneath her bonnet. "Bless you. I can't believe you put yourself at risk, Mister…?"

"Jones. Rafe Jones."

She gave her reticule a squeeze. "My daily receipts are still there. I am truly indebted to you."

The young man at her side was rubbing the back of his neck. "Guns? Whoa, there. Why did this man have your reticule, Aunt Cora?"

Aunt, then, not a mother. Rafe nodded slowly as the woman explained what had happened to her nephew. He became aware of the strike of snow on his back. The flakes were coming faster now, falling like a veil between them.

He considered Miss Cora Sims. He could see the resemblance to the young girl he'd left safely in a hotel room at the other end of town. Both had an appearance of sugary goodness, a feminine softness. What had happened? Holly had been abandoned by her mother as a baby. Cora wore no wedding ring on her slender hand and no widow's weeds. That made him think she'd not left the girl because of some complications in her marriage or a widow's hardship. What, then? What had made this seemingly nice lady give up a child? It had to have been for a good reason, and no easy decision. He felt a rare squeeze of emotion.

Sympathy? He couldn't think of a time when he'd felt much for anyone. A weakness—that was all feelings were. He drew his spine straight and steeled his heart. Time to put some distance between him and his quarry.

"I spoke to the sheriff, but you might want to stop by and add your account of things." He tipped his hat, already walking away. "Good evening to you both."

"Mr. Jones! Wait!" She took a step toward him. The wind swirled the snow between them. It was falling ever harder now. "Do you have family in town? Or are you here for supplies?"

"No family, ma'am, and I don't live in these parts. Just passin' through."

"Come have supper with us. I insist." She swiped snow from her lashes. "This proves no good deed goes unpunished." She smiled.

"I don't need any sort of a reward, ma'am." The rugged man shrouded by storm and shadow cracked a hint of a grin.

"'Ma'am' makes me feel ancient. I'm Miss Cora Sims."

"Miss Sims." He repeated her name, studying her.

Again, that odd sensation swept over her. This man had a powerful presence, not good or bad but simply powerful. The faint light from the store windows offered a dim impression of his face. He was carved granite and toughness. His cheekbones were high and spoke of some Indian blood. His nose was a straight unyielding blade, and his eyes dark pools too mysterious to read.

She nudged her nephew. "This is Eli. Eli, please help persuade Mr. Jones to join us."

Eli, bless him, stepped up. "Mr. Jones, we sure would be honored to have you join us. I know that my brother, as soon as he hears what's happened, will be wantin' to meet you, too."

She felt the man's gaze sharpen. His mouth remained an unsmiling line, but there was kindness in his rugged face. He was a stranger who had put himself at risk to help her. A bad man didn't do things like that.

"All right." His baritone sounded as cold as the coming night. "I can't stay long."

"I won't blame you there." Pleased, she smiled at him—but strictly cordially. She did not want to frighten him off, as she had done with every other bachelor in town.

Oh, it wasn't her smile that did it, she knew, but merely the plain brown look of her. She drew her sash more snugly around her waist to keep out the blast of the rising wind. "You might come to regret having supper with an old maid and her nephews, but we will try not to bore you overly much. I promise."

"That won't be a problem, ma'am—Miss Sims," he corrected with a wry crook of the left side of his mouth. "I worry you'll regret inviting a man like me along."

"Little chance of that," she assured him with all the sincerity she had. It startled her, though, as she took up Eli's arm again, that the man still looked every bit as dangerous as a seasoned outlaw. The kindness she sensed in him didn't soften him one iota. "I never judge a book by its cover for that has happened far too much to me."

He gave her a brief nod, his right eyebrow arching in what might have been faint surprise. He'd probably reckoned that he, a man with guns holstered at his hips, would never have one thing in common with a sensible, brown bird of a spinster.

"This way," Eli said, leading them down the boardwalk, through the snow and into the warm shelter of the town's finest hotel.

Cora couldn't remember the last time she'd had so many people gaping at her. Not even when she'd taken in the boys and rumors had speculated that they were not her nephews but her out-of-wedlock children. She'd had quite a lot of notoriety at the time.

"This is lovely," she told Emmett, who rose from the far end of the table. "You shouldn't have gone to such trouble!"

"It's no trouble for you." Emmett didn't smile. Anyone could see he was sizing up the intruder.

"This is Mr. Jones." She could see how her nephew might get the wrong impression. At first glance Mr. Jones could be mistaken for an outlaw. "I invited him to dine with us. And no—" she'd caught the telling look in Eli's gaze as he opened his mouth to explain "—we shall not speak of what happened. All is well that ends well, thanks to our guest of honor."

Emmett raised a questioning eyebrow but said no more. Eli nodded, blew out a sigh and went for Cora's chair.

"Allow me," Mr. Jones's low voice rumbled kindly, and it was an attractive combination of steeliness, man and goodness. He towered over her so closely, she could see the texture of the day's growth on his jaw. His eyes, which had looked as black as a starless midnight sky, were dark gray.

"Th-thank you." Her words caught in her throat. She was aware of his masculinity, his sheer, towering size and strength. He made her feel small and delicate for the first time in her life. Her face felt hot. Was she blushing? She settled onto the chair and he lingered. She felt the rove of his gaze across her face like a gentle caress.

My, but he was not like any other man she'd met. Rough and intimidating on the outside, but pure gentleman beneath. Her pulse thudded so loudly she hardly realized the background conversations in the room had dropped to whispers as Mr. Jones helped her to scoot her chair in closer to the table.

Her senses sharpened, making her aware of every detail. The scrape of the chair against the wood floor. The splotches of melting snow on his black jacket. The faint scent of winter and high-country air that clung to him. The broad, scarred hands that gripped her chair. The sheen of light on the polished handles of his revolvers. The whisper of his movements as he straightened.

The hushed conversations grew fainter until silence echoed around the well-appointed room. She felt the prickle of many eyes on her. The attention wasn't exactly what she was used to.

Apparently Mr. Jones had something of a reputation.

"Excuse me, sir." Frederick Bauer, the hotel owner, filled the space between her chair and Rafe's. "You should have checked your guns at the door. Hotel policy."

"I didn't know." His voice deepened, radiating power.

What was it about this man? She could not tear her interest away from him, noticing his deliberate, controlled movements. There was no show of anger or annoyance as he loosened the holster's buckle. The left corner of his mouth eased upward a tiny notch, so briefly she wondered if she'd imagined it.

She felt comfortable with him and there was no earthly explanation why. It was as if she had known Mr. Jones all her life. As he handed over his gun belt, she happened to notice he wore no wedding ring.

Mr. Bauer spoke, but his words came as if from a great distance. "I'm sorry to have troubled your guest, Miss Sims. Good evening to you."

"Yes," she said vaguely, hardly aware of the hotel owner's footsteps in the stifling silence. Mr. Jones settled into the chair at her side. All his attention—every last drop of it—seemed intensely on her.

"Sorry about that." Rafe Jones didn't look apologetic. "I forgot I had them on."

"You must be a lawman," Emmett said from across the table.

"A bounty hunter." Mr. Jones went completely still, fastening her with his gaze. "Miss Sims, now that you know, do you want me to leave?"

That was something a bad man would not ask. She felt the impact of his charcoal-gray gaze all the way down to her heart. "No, of course not. It is an honor to have you."

His eyes searched hers, as if measuring her sincerity. His countenance softened, as if he had made his conclusion. "Then I'm glad to be here. How long have you lived in this town?"

"Ten years. It's hard to believe. It seems like yesterday. I came here to Angel Falls to make a new start."

"A new start?"

"Yes, I—" She never finished. Three women had wound their way through the dining room. Joanna McKaslin led the way, with her sister-in-law, Noelle, holding her arm. They were two of Cora's good friends. A younger woman, Matilda, had trailed after them. All carried festively wrapped gifts.

"Happy birthday," they said almost in unison. Noelle, who was blind, turned toward Cora with perfect precision to add with a sweet grin, "Happy *thirtieth* birthday."

"Oh, you *did* have to mention that." Cora's face flamed, but at least it brought back her senses. It wasn't as if she ought to be noticing Mr. Jones's left hand, wedding ring or not. It would be best to concentrate on her guests. Young Matilda, close to Emmett's age, was lovely and shy, and she hesitated over which seat to take. Perhaps she could encourage the young couple's affections. "Emmett, please help Matilda with her chair."

Her nephew was the perfect gentleman as he stood, attentive but reserved, and held out the nearest chair for Matilda. "Miss Worthington, let me help you."

"Why, thank you." A quiet smile faintly shaped the young woman's lips as she slipped into her seat and blushed prettily.

Perfect, Cora thought. There was a chance for the two of them yet. Hope left her beaming, but it was the man at her side who captured her curiosity. He offered faint nods of welcome to the women Eli introduced to him. She couldn't help observing Mr. Jones, while his attention was elsewhere.

He sat straight and strong in his chair, looking as unmovable as a mountain and giving no sign of emotion. Did he regret coming here? She couldn't hazard a guess. He was older than her by several years, she decided, for time had marked his face with pleasant crinkles in the corners of his eyes. He had a maturity that could only come with years of experience.

Not that she was admiring him, goodness no, but perhaps her lonely heart ached with the smallest wish. Impossible, she knew, but there all the same.

"Are you married?" Noelle asked innocently, and it was easy to see her motive.

Cora's face flamed even hotter. She adored her friend, but was Noelle hoping to play matchmaker?

"Never found a woman who would have me." He shifted in his chair, no longer a remote mountain of a man.

"Does that mean you would marry if you found a woman who would lower her standards?" Joanna's gentle kidding was not well veiled, either. The women were trying to marry her off.

"That's not likely to happen. I'm difficult on purpose." He was about as comfortable sitting here now as he would have been walking barefoot through a snake den. He glanced over his shoulder.

"Mr. Jones, are you planning your escape already?" Cora seemed gently amused.

"Nah. Just old habit. I never feel safe with my back to the door."

"I would have thought it was the conversation. I know talk of marriage can make a bachelor mighty uneasy."

"Not much troubles me, Miss Sims." Aside from being vulnerable. He wasn't one for fuss and fancy; he stuck out like a sore thumb. He was here because it was a golden chance. The more he learned about Cora now, the less surveillance he'd have to do later. No way would he hand Holly over to a stranger without answers to some tough questions. He'd best get down to business before the hotel owner returned and asked him to leave. He was making plenty of the other customers nervous.

"What about you?" he asked. A waiter began circling their table unloading glasses of icy water from a fancy silver tray. "It's only fair that I ask why you aren't married."

"Me?" She blinked. Surprise turned to mirth. Her eyes sparkled like jewels, changing her prettiness to a deeper loveliness. "I thought it would be obvious."

"Not to me." She was nice-looking and kind. What kind of man wouldn't want her for his wife?

"There are plenty of reasons." She dismissed the seriousness of his question with a wave of her slender hand. The waiter stepped between them and set down those water glasses. "I suppose you and I have something else in common. I've never met a man who will have me."

The waiter moved on and Rafe caught a flash of sadness in Cora's light blue eyes. The poor lady. He felt as if he'd been gut-punched. A child out of wedlock, even given away, would mark a goodly woman. It would be a sound reason for many men not to take her as a bride. Or for a shy, proper lady not to accept any man's courtship.

"It was because of us," the younger nephew answered. "Aunt Cora denies it, but—"

"Of course I do, because it is utter nonsense. You two are not to blame. Why, you both mean the world to me. Think how lonely I would have been without the two of you coming into my life. Raising you both has been a privilege. One I am truly grateful for."

Rafe didn't doubt that one bit. Even a rough like him could see the gentle sincerity shining within her like the finest of pearls. He'd never seen such sincerity. Honest love rang in the soft notes of her voice. It transformed her into the greatest beauty he'd ever seen.

"We are the ones who are grateful." The oldest nephew spoke up, quick to defend his aunt, or to cover up her sad secret. "We were a handful. No man would want to take us on."

"We were terrors," Eli agreed. "Good thing Aunt Cora set us straight, but we did scare off every eligible suitor."

"You both saved me from a world of loneliness. There is nothing more important than family and nothing more important than love. Now, enough of this talk of me. Matilda, how is your new sewing project coming along?"

Rafe could sense her sadness. He could breathe it in like a foggy morning. There was no man on a string, no possible husband around the corner, no lurid past she might want to stay in denial about. She was too loving a lady to have left her own helpless out-of-wedlock newborn at an orphanage.

The waiter approached to take their orders. Too late. Rafe had lost all appetite. He had no doubt that gentle, loving Cora Sims with her pretty dress shop, her caring friends and her well-raised nephews was hiding a great tragedy in her past. One too painful to face? He could not know without asking more.

He hunted outlaws for a living. He'd seen it all. Every kind of conscienceless murderer and rapist and thief. He hated that something so horrid had touched this fine woman. Suddenly this job took a bad turn. What was the right thing to do? Was it right to bring up a terrible memory for this kind woman? He clenched his jaw until his back teeth ached. What if he was about to destroy this woman's happiness?

Worse, what about Holly? What if she didn't get the mother she was hoping for? He grabbed up his menu and stared at it. Maybe the girl had constructed that story of her ma leaving her, needing to believe it. He knew how that was, too. One endless day followed by another in an orphanage without love and gentleness of any kind could destroy a child. You had to believe in something to hold on.

Look at him. He was all tied up and hurting something fierce. This was what giving in to feelings got a man. He took a long swallow of cold water and glanced around the fancy dining room, feeling out of place and out of luck, and not only for himself.

Chapter Three

Snow drifted lazily through the nighttime air as Cora ambled down the hotel steps. "Thank you all. I can't remember ever having a more enjoyable time."

"It was our pleasure," Joanna assured her with a warm hug. "We've stayed much later than we expected. There's my husband, standing watch for us. He's come to see us home."

Cora waved at the quiet, stoic man standing next to his team of horses at the hitching post. It was too far away to call out. The town was quite crowded tonight. There was a spelling bee over at the schoolhouse, and the overflow of horses and vehicles were lined up along the street. After waving off Noelle, Matilda and Joanna, Cora turned to her nephews. Goodness, but it was difficult saying goodbye to those two.

"I'll stop by the store tomorrow," Emmett promised. "To see if you need me to do any deliveries for you."

"You are far too busy to run errands for me." She was

proud of him; he was a fine young man for thinking of her. "Eli, I expect to see you in church on Sunday?"

"Yes, ma'am." Eli had a habit of sleeping in on Sunday mornings. She pinched his cheek affectionately, hating that the boys glanced at each other with a look she recognized well. They were deciding which would have the burden of seeing her home. Not that they saw her as a burden, but they were young men with far better things to do than fuss over her.

"I'll do the honors." Mr. Jones stepped out of the shadows, looking every bit as dark and shadowed as the criminals he tracked. "Miss Sims?"

The interest he showed her, the offer he made and the buttery richness of his tone made her heart wedge painfully between her ribs. Was it possible that he had decided to court her? No man, aside from family, had ever escorted her home.

"Why, thank you. That would be nice." She fell into step with him. He felt substantial, like a man who could do anything. He felt like honor and goodness. Her knees wobbled a trifle as she walked at his side. The last image of her nephews was of their wide, smiling faces. They were already leaping to conclusions.

Certainly Mr. Jones was not interested in her. He was merely being a gentleman. She concentrated on making her feet connect properly with the boardwalk. Although she was officially off the shelf, she didn't feel thirty years old. She felt eighteen again, with her life before her and full of wonderful possibilities.

"I hope I'm heading in the right direction."

"Yes. I live a street over from the library at the end

of the boardwalk." It was ahead of them, past shop windows closed for the night. The falling snow fell like a veil, disguising the route ahead. It felt private walking at his side. "You said you were passing through. Do you often come here for supplies?"

"I hail from the Dakotas, mostly."

"Mostly? Surely you have a home somewhere."

"I've spent most of my life living out of my saddlebags."

"Your job must require that."

"Not necessarily as much as I do." He kept his pace slow to accommodate her. "It's a way of life I've gotten used to."

"Do you like it?"

"Not much. Always thought I might like to be a gunsmith. Buy myself a building and settle in one place. Never have done it, though."

"You and I have the exact opposite lives." She dodged an ice patch, her skirts swishing with her movements. "I have stayed in exactly the same place all day long, all year long for the better part of a decade."

"You ever want to hop aboard the train and take off for parts unknown?"

"More than you can imagine, but that is not the proper thing for a lady to do."

"No, it's a dangerous world." She was a surprise. He never would have figured her for an adventurer, even if only in daydreams. "You said you moved here for a new start."

"Isn't that the reason everyone moves West? A chance to start over and leave the mistakes of the past behind?"

"And the sorrows."

"Yes, those, too."

He thought of his own sadness best left forgotten. He hated doing it, but he had to pry. Asking her was the most respectful way to do it. He could go back to Miles City and dig up her sorrowful past without her consent or knowledge. He steeled his spine, determined to do his job. "What sorrow could a pretty lady like you have?"

"I buried my mother, followed by my younger sister." She turned somber, as quiet as the night. "Scarlet fever. Before that, my father was lost in the war."

"You must have been very young."

"I was eleven when my father died, seventeen when my mother died, a year older when my sister passed."

"I'm sorry." He made himself as cold as the snow falling on the boards at his feet and did his best not to think of this nice lady burying the last of her family. He cleared every trace of emotion from his voice. "Were you alone? Did you have someone to look out for you? To protect you?"

"No one." Sadness sifted over her like the snow on her bonnet. Emotions played across her face, and even in the shadows it was easy to see she did not give in to sorrow. "I sold our house and the last plot of land and boarded the stagecoach. When we stopped here in Angel Falls to take on passengers, I liked the friendly look of the town, and the countryside seemed pleasant. I didn't bother to travel any farther. I knew in my heart I had found the new start I had been praying for."

"You were young to move to a strange town on your own. Weren't you lonely?"

"I joined the church and made friends."

"But you left everything you had ever known. Why, exactly?"

"Everywhere I looked there were memories of the people I loved, who were gone. I felt terribly alone."

"Why didn't you choose to marry, instead of heading off?"

"I never had a beau. I was too young and sheltered." The darkness enveloped her, as if helping her to keep her secrets.

So, that eliminated a love match gone wrong and the shame of an out-of-wedlock child. He guided her down the steps at the end of the boardwalk and into the snowy street. He could not see enough of her face to guess more. "But you have lived here a good length of time. You could have chosen to marry."

"Oh, not marrying was never my choice."

He couldn't imagine it. "Thick-skulled men must live in this town."

"I have always thought so."

He changed sides to take the brunt of the brutal north wind and caught a glimpse of her smile. Something about her tugged at him—sympathy. That was what it was. That was all it could be.

The road they had turned down was one long stretch of homes huddled beneath barren trees. The glow from windows glinted and shone on the falling snow. It was a pleasant night with their footsteps a hush in the music of the snowfall. It was pleasant having her at his side.

"What about you, Mr. Jones?"

Her question startled him. He wasn't used to accompanying women along town streets or conversing with them. He was on unfamiliar ground. "There's not much to tell."

"What about your family?"

"I have none."

"No family? Not anywhere?" Her dulcet, gentle voice was like the sun dawning.

He was like the night. So why did he find himself leaning toward her? Why did he answer? "I have a ward. Her name is Holly."

"You are not alone, then. I'm glad. You're a good man, Mr. Jones, and you don't deserve a solitary life."

His conscience winced. She was an innocent type who probably saw good in everyone. "You don't know me, Miss Sims."

"I can see more than you might think. You stop to help a stranger and then you return her reticule."

"It was nothing." And not without motive. Luck had oddly favored him tonight. "Truth is, I was watching you earlier and I saw what happened. I was too far away to come to your aid, but I could hunt the thief down. I could have left your reticule at the sheriff's office, but I wanted to meet you."

"Oh." She blushed. "I'm glad you did, so I could thank you. I hope you enjoyed the meal tonight. You were uncomfortable."

"Did it show?"

"Only a bit. I don't think anyone else noticed."

"I'm not used to crystal and silver. I'm more of a tin-and-steel sort."

"There's nothing wrong with that."

Perhaps some would say Mr. Jones was rough around the edges and quite disreputable-looking, but she was charmed. She had never felt quite this way before, as if she were dancing on spun sugar. "Then I'm keeping you from your ward," she said. "You should have said something. She could have joined us."

"Maybe another time."

"I would like that." She dragged her feet, slowing. They had reached her walkway. If only their time together could continue; it had passed so quickly. "Tell me about your little Holly."

"She's ten years old. Yay high." He gestured with his hand. "Small for her age." He came to a stop beside her and held up his free hand. "She can talk a tail off a mule."

"How long have you been raising her?"

"Not long. It's new to me. All of it."

"I know that feeling well." She recognized the sincere concern on Rafe Jones's rugged face. "When my nephews first came to live with me, I was lost. I didn't know what I was doing."

"Yep, that's how it is." He smiled. In the dark shadows, his brief smile was breathtaking. His hard face softened. "She needs a home and I'm not a settling-down kind of man."

"Then what are you going to do?"

"Get her a home."

"I'm sure you will manage just fine." She pulled her house key from her reticule. "Love for them gives us strength. It surely guided me through the years. I think the boys have turned out well."

"You have done a fine job with them."

"And you will do the same for your girl." She knew it was true.

A hint of his smile remained, softening the hard look of him. Although it was too dark to be sure, he seemed to watch her carefully. As if with interest.

Hope beat painfully, afraid to take flight. She had been disappointed many times before. Did she say good-night while she was still ahead? Before he realized she really was as plain as she looked?

"I'll be staying around awhile." He reached out and brushed a snowflake from her eyelash with the pad of his thumb. A tender act.

Sweetness sifted through her. "Then perhaps I will be seeing you again, Mr. Jones."

"I'm sure of it." He tipped his hat to her, the way any suitor would. "Good night, Miss Sims."

"Good night." Her knees wobbled again as she forced her feet to carry her up the walkway. Snow crunched beneath her shoes, but she could hardly hear it for her heart's drumming. Her cheek still tingled from his brief touch.

Thank you, Father, for bringing Mr. Jones into my life. Please watch over him this night.

As she slipped the key into the lock and gave it a turn, she glanced over her shoulder to catch sight of the man striding away. He was shrouded in shadows and lost to the dark, so there was only the faintest outline of him at the street's end, strong of shoulder and powerfully intimidating. She no longer felt like a thirty-year-old spinster, washed-up and past her prime.

What a fine birthday present!

If she never saw Mr. Jones again, she thanked him for that.

Softer feelings would have stuck with him if he had let them. Rafe tromped up the back stairs, shedding snow as he went. He didn't care for how he was about to change Cora Sims's life. He was certain there could be only one reason a nice lady like her would leave a baby. A terrible injustice had been done her when she had been alone and unprotected, and as soon as she had the baby—Holly—Cora had moved to this peaceful little town to forget and start fresh.

He felt sorry for her. That was what the tug of emotion was, nothing more. He couldn't see what to do next. His gut was all twisted up over this quandary. He unlocked his door and shrugged out of his coat.

The door to the next room was ajar and the fall of light drew his eye through the dark. A few steps forward and he could see the girl in her worn-thin flannel nightgown kneeling beside her bed. Her patched flannel cap crowned her bowed head, and all he could see was the shine of her long, honey-gold hair—very similar to Cora's.

He felt an unfamiliar twist in his chest. Yep, Cora Sims was one fine woman. Nothing like many proper women who took one look and cast him in the same lot as outlaws. No, when Cora looked at him with that kind way of hers, he felt ten feet tall. Like the man he wished he could be. He hung up his hat and sat down on the bed. The sagging ropes gave a halfhearted squeak beneath his weight as he pulled off his boots.

Holly was still praying. He could see her hands folded as she chattered on to God. If God listened to anyone, Rafe was fairly sure He would listen to that girl. She sure could rattle on and make a man smile.

"And bless my ma," Holly went on, fast as a speeding locomotive, "cuz she had to leave me and she might be awful lonely. I know I sure am. I don't care if she don't got much, and does she like to make pancakes? Mostly please, please, please, God, make her love me."

Rafe set his boots aside, his chest tighter than it had ever been. He leaned a shoulder against the doorjamb and nodded once to the elderly woman—the hotel owner's ma, Mrs. Plymouth—who was sitting in the far corner of the room.

"And most of all, God, please bless Mr. Rafe. I got my ma, but he don't got no one."

That was new. He'd never been prayed for before. He cleared his throat to let the girl know he was home. Her prayer became a blur of words that ended with a breathless "amen." She bounced to her feet and thundered across the floorboards.

"Mr. Rafe! Did you find her? Did you?" The girl danced in place, bobbing with excitement.

It couldn't be good for her to get all worked up like that. He scowled at the hope bubbling out of the girl. Hope was a false promise, something that didn't exist. He sure hoped she wasn't headed for a hard fall. "I'll let you know when to start hoping. I told you it will take time."

He thought of Cora standing alone on her front step.

He'd felt comfortable talking with her. That was odd. He wasn't a man who spent much time in a lady's company. Maybe it had something to do with the fact that she hadn't looked at him as if he belonged on the wrong side of town.

He rubbed the back of his neck, troubled. He couldn't get the look of her out of his head, or the jeweled honesty he'd seen in her eyes. He kept remembering how her complexion was porcelain fine and how her rosebud mouth was usually gently smiling.

"I know, but it's awful hard to wait. I love my ma so much. She ain't gonna be nothin' like Mrs. Beams."

He took in those big eyes with their shining expectation and stepped back into the shadows, where he felt safer, where he belonged. "You're only going to make it tough on yourself, getting your hopes up. If things don't work out, they are going to come crashing right down. Do you hear?"

"Y-yes, s-sir." She blinked hard against the pooling tears. "I didn't mean to get excited. I just love my ma so much."

The girl didn't even *know* her ma. He rubbed his neck again and blew out a sigh. It didn't help. The tangle was still in his gut. "You go to sleep and we'll see what morning brings. I'm tired of those rags you keep wearing. Tomorrow we'll go get you some new things."

"Okay." She was still blinking as she padded toward her open door. "Good night, Mr. Rafe."

"Night." He stayed still a moment or two with his eyes closed, trying to make the coiled knot in his midsection relax. There wasn't a chance of that, so he paced to the window and eased back the curtains.

As he gazed out over the dark street and the steady snowfall, he listened to the bed ropes creak as Mrs. Plymouth tucked the girl into bed. There was low conversation, some murmurings. He didn't pay attention to it as he drew out his wallet and counted out enough greenbacks for the sitter. He kept his feelings as cold as the frozen world outside, numb to the beauty of the falling snow and to the houses tucked in for the night, lamplight glowing like cozy squares of tranquillity.

Somewhere out there was Cora's house. He thought of her safely locked behind closed doors, maybe making a cup of tea and sitting down to do some needlework before bedtime. The tangle within him became a cold, steady pain. He didn't know what it was about the woman, but she was starlight next to his shadows. He let the curtain fall closed, feeling more sorely alone than he could ever remember feeling.

Chapter Four

Cora couldn't remember a busier morning. She was bundling up a few basting jobs for Joanna, who sewed for her, when the bustle in the shop seemed to still. The pleasant din of conversation faded. She felt one side of her face prickle, as if remembering Rafe Jones's slight touch. When the bell above the door jingled, she already knew who was approaching her shop with the confident sound of boots and jangle of spurs.

Rafe Jones. He was black from head to toe. Black duster jacket. Black Stetson. Black gloves. Black shirt and trousers. The shop fell silent as he perched in the open doorway, his guns at his hips. Behind him lurked a thin slip of a child with eyes too big for her narrow, peaked face.

His ward. Holly. The pair of them moved into the shop, and Cora softened at once. The poor thing looked as if she'd been half starved and worked too hard, and not that long ago. The delicate skin beneath the girl's eyes looked bruised, and she appeared to be all bones. When Rafe had said he hadn't been in charge of her for long, he'd obviously meant it. *Lord, please bless that man.*

"Look who it is," Joanna whispered, seeming terribly pleased. "He must really like you to walk into a dress shop. Most of the men in town won't do it."

"I'll see you later." Cora winked, refusing to say more. No doubt Joanna had plenty of ideas of her own. She skirted the edge of the counter. "Mr. Jones. Welcome."

"Good to see you." He tipped his hat to her, watching her with little show of emotion.

Probably due to the dozen curious women who stared openly at him. His strong shoulders were braced, and he looked quite untroubled by the attention. Then again, he was a brave man, used to holding his own with outlaws. A women's dress shop might not intimidate him overly much. She liked that about him.

"You must be Holly," she said to the little girl.

"Yes'm." Holly bobbed her head and kept close to her protector. "Mr. Rafe, you sure they got dresses for me here?"

"Pretty sure," he rumbled.

The shop seemed less silent as Cora held out her hand to the girl. "I can't think that Mr. Jones knows a lot about dresses. Would you like me to help you find what you need?"

Big blue eyes widened. She nodded once, the only sign of consent.

"That's it? Cat got your tongue?" Amusement

curved the corners of Rafe's mouth. The sun chose that moment to break out between storm clouds, casting him in a golden ray of light that came through the window. "All the way here, she about talked both my ears off."

"I'm sure she and I will find plenty to say, don't you worry. What did you need for her today?"

"Everything." He took off his hat and stared at the brim. "We've been on the road. Haven't had much time for buying anything but necessities."

"I can take care of that. Did you want to stay? I have coffee keeping warm on the stove. Or you can come back in an hour or so. That will give us time to find what she needs."

"That's right kind of you. I can see you're busy."

"For you, I don't mind. Holly, there's a basket of candy right on the counter. Why don't you help yourself."

"Really?" Pleasure put color into her face. "Thank you, ma'am!"

Unmistakable affection melted the iciness of the man's gaze. He might look dangerous, Cora thought, but she suspected Mr. Jones had a soft heart. She was pleased that with all the other shops in town offering children's clothing, he had chosen hers. As the girl trotted up to the counter, she turned to him. "How much were you looking to spend? I don't want to surprise you with the bill."

"A hundred. That enough?"

"I can get her plenty for that. How long will you be staying in town?"

"Depends."

"My inventory of girls' dresses has been picked over. This is my busiest time of the year."

"I don't want frills for her. Good, sensible clothes." He appeared aloof, with his hands fisted loosely at his sides, but he watched her as if she were the most interesting woman on earth.

My, that was definitely unusual. His scrutiny befuddled her brain and made her pulse rickety. Rafe Jones seemed intensely serious as he swept his hat back on his head and met her gaze with unapologetic frankness.

"I'll be back inside an hour," he said. "I'll look forward to seeing you again, Cora."

Not "Miss Sims," now. There was no deferring politeness in his tone that she was used to receiving from all the other men in town. No, Rafe Jones tipped his hat to her and smiled, giving her a hint of dimples before he turned on his heel and stalked out the door.

Her heart rolled over in one slow, painful movement.

"I like that man." Joanna was at her side, speaking low. "He means business."

"You mean courting business." Saying those words aloud felt like inviting bad luck. She had placed her hopes on a man's attentions before. Still, there was something different about Rafe's attentions. "Remember the rancher out at the edge of town who was only interested in a convenient wife for his children? He thought I would be interested, being so old, as he phrased it. Then there was Mr. Landry, who thought I wanted to help him run his pig farm. He figured the sale of my shop would give him the funds he needed to make his payments to the bank."

"Those men were never interested in *you*." Joanna turned to watch the man cross the street. "Mr. Jones seems quite taken. He cannot keep his eyes off you. Mark my words, he's sweet on you. Is that his daughter?"

"His ward." It took effort not to watch the confident stride of the man weaving between traffic toward the gunsmith's shop. The girl had unwrapped a piece of candy and was sucking on it carefully and gazing wistfully at the display case full of colorful ribbons. Cora realized she hadn't asked if Holly was his niece or some other relation. There was a whole volume of things she didn't know about the man.

"Let me know how it goes." Joanna smiled broadly as she tied her bonnet ribbons. "I want a full report. My guess is that Mr. Jones stays in town longer than expected to start courting you."

"It's more likely he will ride on out of town and not miss me one bit." That was the practical side of her talking, the side that had learned to carefully protect herself. It was entirely too easy to get her heart broken. "I'll see you tomorrow, Joanna."

"I'm keeping you in my prayers."

Cora waited until her friend was out the door before she headed over to the girl. "Do you like hair ribbons?"

"Yes'm. I used to have two sets to match my dresses. My pa bought 'em for me."

Two sets. Not a lot by her customers' standards. Cora held out her hand. "Let us go take a look at the dresses in the back. When we find what you like, we can match some hair ribbons to them. How does that sound?"

"Mighty fine." Pretty blue eyes lit up, bringing the child alive. She was cute, with a round cherub's face, an uptilted nose and delicate bone structure. She would grow into quite a beauty. Her blond hair, which curled out of her twin braids, was mostly hidden beneath a sagging wool hat.

Cora took the girl's small hand and led her through the aisles of fabrics and accessories and shoppers. She was glad for the part-time help she had hired. She checked on her workers, who looked busy but not unmanageably so, and went straight to the girls' dresses.

"Something practical." Cora considered the half-dozen frocks that were about Holly's size. She pushed aside the party silks and velveteens trimmed with seed pearls and imported lace, and considered the plainest dress on the rod. A warm-green wool, princess-style dress with satin ribbons and mother-of-pearl buttons.

"It don't got no ruffles or puffy sleeves." The girl's comment was a quiet one, especially compared to the privileged young lady one aisle over who was in a tantrum over the expensive bonnet she wanted. "I sure like ruffles and puffy sleeves."

"The other dresses are for fancy parties, not for everyday." Cora kept her tone gentle. She understood what it was like to have impractical wishes. "I don't suppose you go to many fancy parties."

"A party? I ain't never been to one of them."

Poor girl. Cora smoothed the golden wisps from the

child's face, feeling oddly tender. It was clear by the look of the girl's ill-fitting calico dress that she needed a woman's care. Not that Rafe wasn't trying. The calico dress seemed new, perhaps purchased at a mercantile, but it was a size too large.

"Why don't you try this dress on? I know it doesn't have puffy sleeves, but feel how soft the fabric is."

Fingers emerged from too-long coat sleeves to stroke the fine-quality wool. She nodded somberly. "It's softer than a kitten."

"I have more fabric just as soft. I can make a few more dresses, if you want."

"With ruffles?"

"And I can make one with puffy sleeves."

"That'd be mighty fine." When Holly smiled, she brightened like the sun at noon. Adorable.

Then again, Cora had a soft spot for children. "I want you to try this on. There's a place behind the curtain to change."

An impatient voice interrupted. "Cora! Cora, I need assistance."

"Of course, Mrs. Bell." She sent a reassuring smile in the wealthy matron's direction before handing Holly the green woolen. "I have a few other customers to wait on, Holly, and then I will help you pick out fabric for your new dresses. Would you like that?"

"Yes'm!" The girl seized the dress and scampered off, such a dear thing and so well mannered.

"Cora." Jessalyn Bell's narrow mouth was pressed into a flat line. Impatience vibrated through her. "I am waiting."

"Yes, Mrs. Bell, I'm coming." When the child tugged one of the curtains closed, Cora rounded the display, turning her attention to one of her more important—and difficult—customers. "How may I help you?"

"A scandal, children like that." Jessalyn shook her head in disapproval, her jowls quivering. "It oughtn't to be allowed."

Cora glanced at the red-faced twelve-year-old stamping her foot in the aisle, Jessalyn's youngest, then at the curtain now pulled closed. "Yes," she said quietly. "It is a scandal when hardship happens to a helpless child. How can I help you?"

While Mrs. Bell went on, oblivious to her daughter's angry display, Cora felt a tingle at her nape. When she glanced over her shoulder, she saw nothing but the expanse of snowy boardwalk and street. No sign of Rafe. She warmed sweetly and let hope fill her—just a little. Maybe she wasn't too old for romance, after all.

The hour was nearly up. Rafe lumbered up the steps onto the boardwalk, wet from the melting snow. He had a good view into Cora's shop. The front windows sparkled without a streak or even a speck of dirt, making it easy to pick her out. Most of the shoppers had left. Two employees appeared busy—one folding up bolts of material, the other tallying up purchases at the counter.

Cora waltzed into sight from the back, where she carried a paper-wrapped bundle in the crook of her arm. She sure looked a sight in that brown-and-white-striped shirt and brown skirt. The colors brought out the gold tones in her hair. He liked the way she had piled it loosely on top of her head, a few curls spilling down to frame her face.

She was sure a fine woman. Not wealthy like some of the women who had filed out of her store. But she was every bit as quality. Maybe more. It was the composed way she held herself, with her spine straight and her movements calm and sure. Her manner of gently respecting everyone.

Yep, he sure liked her, and that spelled trouble. He juggled the bags and opened the door. The bell overhead jingled a merry welcome, making Cora look up. He steeled himself. Whatever it took, he could not let her smile thaw him. He had a job to do. A job, nothing more.

A child caught hold of his sleeve and held on tight. "Mr. Rafe, look at what I got. Miss Sims is gonna make me up more dresses."

Holly. He hardly recognized her. Her green dress complemented her blue eyes and gold hair. Not the spitting image of the woman setting the package on the counter, but close enough.

"I ought to be finished sewing by the end of next week at the latest." Cora circled the counter, efficiently pulling a pad from her pocket and a pencil from the countertop.

The way she moved captivated him. It was like watching the stars dance through a midwinter sky. She was like the North Star, hovering in place, the anchor for all the others. He certainly felt drawn to her and couldn't turn away.

"I hope that will be all right." She jotted a few things on the notepad. "Since you haven't told me precisely how long you are staying in town."

"Until Christmas." That was news to him. He didn't know why he said it. He hadn't given it much thought. "At least, that's what I reckon."

"Good. The candlelight service on Christmas Eve is always touching. We have a wonderful, down-to-earth minister. I don't know if you are a churchgoing man."

"Used to be." Back when he was young, when he still could believe. Life had stripped him of that belief.

"Is there singin'?" Holly released his sleeve and padded toward Cora. "I sure do like singin'."

"Yes. We do a lot of singing. There is a church organ and a choir, too."

"My pa used to preach on Sundays. That was, until he fell sick."

He would have to be deaf not to hear the sad longing in the girl's voice. The ice around his heart cracked. He couldn't stand to hear more of her sad story. It was none of his business. She'd hired him with the few pennies she had—not that he'd taken them yet or planned to. She was a job, nothing more. No sense getting all caught up in emotions when a parting of ways was certain. A smart man would remember that. What he should do is get a few more of his questions answered, break the news to Cora and ride south to warmer weather.

"You must miss your pa something terrible." Cora abandoned her tablet and leaned down so that she was eye to eye with Holly. Concern wreathed her lovely face and it was easy to see what she was made of.

"I know how much it hurts." She wiped a tear from the girl's cheek. "I lost my pa when I wasn't much older than you."

"You did? Did you hafta go to an orphanage, too?"

"No, I still had my mother to take care of me and my sister. Is that what happened to you?"

"Uh-huh. I don't ever wanna go back."

"Then you must be thankful for Mr. Jones." She brushed the last tear from the girl's cheek. "He takes good care of you."

"Yep, but he don't know much about girls. He can't help it none."

"But he tries."

Thank heaven for responsible, caring men like Rafe Jones, Cora thought. "Did you want to pick out the ribbons now, Holly?"

"Yes'm." The girl padded off, the skirt of her dress swirling around her knees. What a good thing Mr. Jones had done, taking the girl in!

I'm not sweet on him, she told herself firmly. She returned to her pencil and finished tallying, but where was her attention? It was on the big man as he set a brown bag on the edge of her counter. The scent of roasted chicken and fresh rye bread wafted from it.

"For you, Cora. You take lunch?"

"Yes. I have a room in the back where I eat."

"Would you mind some company?"

"I would love some." She did her best to keep her smile from showing. Any moment now she would start to believe that he really was still interested in her. Her heart would be in jeopardy. Where was her common sense when she needed it?

"Then it's settled," he said. He set down the second bag he carried, perhaps his and Holly's sandwiches. For a moment his gaze lingered and there was something in his eyes she had never seen before. At least not for her.

Caring. Affection. Those rare, beautiful emotions lingered for a brief moment, then vanished. Holly was calling to him, asking how many ribbons she could have.

He backed away and put distance between them, but she did not forget. Sweetness filled her as she watched the big man kneel to talk quietly to the girl. The tender tones wrapped about Cora like hope. She did not forget the affection she'd glimpsed. It took all her strength to keep her wishes reined in and her feet firmly on the ground.

Chapter Five

The back door shut quietly as Holly escaped to play in the alley, leaving Cora alone with the man in black. Snow was gently falling as she poured two cups of steaming tea to finish their meal. Rafe Jones was not an easy man to ignore. His presence seemed to shrink the comfortable room.

"What made you become a seamstress?" he asked, watching her with frank intensity.

Her face heated. He'd had plenty of time with her, enough to know that she wasn't interesting, witty or engaging. He didn't seem to mind. That made her like him more.

"After my father's death, my mother sold off the horses and parceled out most of the land, giving us money enough to survive for a time. But after all the valuables were sold and the money ran out, my mother did piecework sewing for a company. She would bring work home and my sister and I would sit beside her and help."

"Your family was rich?"

"We had been comfortable. But material things have little value in the end. How could they? They are so easily lost. I would have gladly traded every jewel and our ten-room house for one more day with my family."

"It's why I've never fussed much about possessions."

"You are a wise man, Rafe." Her boldness at the use of his Christian name surprised her, but he didn't seem to mind.

"Hardly."

She dropped two lumps of sugar into her tea and stirred. It gave her time to observe more about him. The way he drank his tea without sugar, and steaming hot. Cradling his cup in one callused hand, he leaned toward her, inclining just enough to make it seem as if no space whatsoever stood between them.

Please, let him keep liking me. The prayer arose without thought, too late to call it back. Ashamed, she took a sip of tea. There were greater woes in the world. Greater sufferings and misfortunes for the Lord to tend to than her romantic hopes. Perhaps she was spending far too much time thinking about her own wishes. "Now it's your turn to answer questions," she said.

"I didn't know we were taking turns."

She smiled even as she willed herself not to. My, what an impact this man made! She felt a fluttering inside, as if her entire spirit were taking wing. How on earth was she going to manage to hold back her feelings? She gazed out the window where Holly was holding out her hands and spinning like the snow. The girl was as safe as could be and having fun.

She took another sip of hot tea. "Why did you become a bounty hunter?"

"I spent most of my early years in an orphanage out of Sioux City. I was seven years old when I was hired out to a farmer. He was a hard man, but I got lucky. He sold me off to another older couple. The husband had fallen too sick to do heavy labor around his homestead."

"You were *sold?* At seven years old?"

"I was nearly eight by then." He took a long swallow of tea. His eyes darkened, as if with cold memories. "It happens all the time. The orphanages have too many children and not enough money."

"I see. I hate to think they are such heartless places."

"They aren't. Just poor." He set down his cup. "You look quite affected by that."

"I've never given it much thought. We have a yearly Christmas drive at the church. We try to help a nearby orphanage." She swiped stray curls from her eyes, staring out the window where the girl played. "Holly was in one."

"She was. When I met her, she was half starved and working twelve-hour days for a woman in Helena."

"She's only ten years old!"

"Old enough to earn her keep, some would say. I'm glad I took her from that."

"Me, too." Tears filled her eyes. "She's such a nice girl."

"She surely is." He couldn't say he wasn't affected by Cora's compassion, the shimmer of tears in her eyes. She had quite a tender heart. Could she have left a newborn in such a place? He couldn't see it. "Have you ever been to one?"

"An orphanage? No."

He believed her. That meant she must have left the baby with caring, adoptive parents. That would explain the man Holly called Pa. There were no records to show he was her real father, not that there were often any. Holly had a family Bible she had managed to hold on to, but there had been no notation of her birth in it.

"Was the older couple nicer to you?" Cora's eyes narrowed, as if she was trying to see past his day's growth and his defenses.

"They were, but after Mr. Tilden recovered from consumption, they couldn't afford to keep me on. I was fourteen by then. I could pass for a few years older. I was tall for my age. I joined the Union Army and fought in the War Between the States."

"You never had a childhood."

"Sure I did." He brushed off her concern; he didn't know what else to do. Tears still stood in her eyes, for him now. It made him uncomfortable. He wasn't used to being looked at like that. When he grabbed up his cup and drained the rest of the tea, he could feel her gaze like the gentlest of touches.

As the tea scorched his gut, he hated to think what she saw. A man in his thirties who had lived a hard life, with time etched on his face and no softness inside.

"My father wrote home faithfully," she said, "and he often told of the soldiers hardly more than boys who had enlisted and who fought beside him." Sympathy. It was right there on her face, plain for him to see.

His chest seized tight. Never had he seen such a thing, and all for him. He stared down at the empty depths of the teacup and found no answer there. He was all tangled up again with no chance for relief. Because if he took off out that door, like his every instinct was telling him to, he would only have to talk to her another time. There were things that needed to be said. Truths that had to be unearthed.

"I fared all right." His words came out scratchy from all the strain of trying not to feel things for her. "When the war was over, I looked for work for a long spell."

"You didn't have any family. Anyone to come home to." She bridged the few feet separating them and laid her hand on his. Her compassionate touch was satin soft.

He closed his eyes, fighting to stay as frozen as the earth in winter. "I did all right. I was handy with a gun, and tracking outlaws suits me."

"You've been alone all this time? Hasn't there been anyone at all?"

Her sympathy chipped away at him. He didn't bother to answer. Didn't see how he could. He'd been alone until that little girl had hired him. He looked out the window where she was at play, intent on rolling up a big ball of snow.

The tangle in his chest nearly choked him. He wanted to say that being around folks was nothing but a complication, a burden, to a wandering soul like him. It wasn't the truth. He was a little sweet on her.

"There has been no one for me, either," she confessed.

So there had been no beau. She withdrew her hand, but the connection between them remained.

"Your life will be changing quite a bit," she said, "now that you have Holly to raise."

"To tell you the truth, I won't be raising her." This was where it got tricky. He drew himself up straighter in his chair, hating to dig up Cora's painful past. "I reckon her ma is alive. I intend to find the lady and leave Holly with her."

"Oh, I hadn't realized." Those tears hovered again, dangerously close to brimming over. "That would be a great blessing, to reunite a mother with her daughter."

He reckoned the woman in front of him might be thinking of the baby she'd left behind. Maybe that accounted for her tears. Then again, Cora did have a generous heart, the most generous he'd ever come across.

"What are you going to do?" she asked. "It will be hard for you to leave Holly behind. You're fond of her."

"I'm used to leaving folks behind. It's why she hired me."

"Hired you?"

"With three pennies. It was the only money she had." A muscle worked in his jaw and he stopped short, as if there was more to say.

"Let me guess." She could see how the tough bounty hunter did not have the strength to say no to a helpless child. "You're passing through town on your way to find the mother."

"Not passing through, no." He laid his hand on hers. She could feel every rough callus just as easily as she could feel his affection. Tenderness glittered in her like stardust.

I cannot be sweet on him, she told herself, not this quick and not without a long courtship, the way love was supposed to come. Love should be the gentle result of time spent together and common wishes. Something reasonable and compatible, not a sudden, unbidden emotion that made every inch of her heart and soul feel and fill, even the unused corners she did not know she had.

A knock on the inside door startled her. A quick look told her that Holly was still playing in the quiet alleyway, rolling snow to make a head for a snowman.

"Excuse me." She hated to move away from him. It was like walking away from paradise. She wondered if Rafe felt the same. His gray eyes had turned charcoal with emotion, and there was no mistaking his gentle regard as he watched her cross the room.

Her heart began to pound. She had given up on romance and it had found her, anyway. God had not forgotten her, although she had lost hope. She opened the inside door, which led into the shop.

Molly, one of her part-time helpers, peered in. "There's a customer asking for you, Cora."

"I'll be right there." Her voice didn't sound like her own. Her words were too happy and far too hopeful. The door to the shop closed, giving them privacy. "My lunchtime is over."

"Then I'll get out of your way." He grabbed his coat and his hat. "I want to talk more with you, Cora."

"I would like that." Rafe was the kind of man she

could talk to forever. He fascinated her. She felt he truly cared when he listened to her. "The store is closed on Sundays."

"Sunday, then." He loaded his arms with the wrapped bundle of Holly's new things. His gaze darkened as he paced closer.

My, but he looked intent. Joanna's words rolled into her mind. *He cannot keep his eyes off you. Mark my words, he's sweet on you.* She smiled shyly as he leaned close, gazing into her eyes for one long moment.

"You are a mighty fine lady, Cora Sims." He moved to the door, but he didn't look as if he wanted to leave.

His words made her resistance tumble. She could no longer deny it. She was sweet on *him*. Of all the men who had crossed her path both here and in Miles City, where she used to live, none had ever affected her like this. "Will you and Holly be attending church?"

"I reckon she will drag me there." The twinkle in his dark eyes said that he didn't mind so much. "Any chance you would want to sit next to me?"

She was foolhardy, that was what she was, liking him far too much. But his steady gentleness made it simple to believe that he felt the same way. "I'd be glad to sit with you."

"How about that?" He hesitated, as if there was more he wanted to say, but he opened the door. Snowflakes tumbled over him, dappling him with their purity, clinging to him like grace. He was more snowflake than shadow. The last thing she saw was his heart in his smile. He closed the door, leaving her alone to weave dreams of him.

* * *

Holly hung back, clinging to the wooden sill of the dry-goods store's display window. To keep her new dress for Sunday, she wore her old clothes, and had a neglected look to her. She needed Cora, Rafe thought, someone who would have enough love to spend on the little things. Like hair ribbons and starched bonnets and perfectly tied sashes.

Too bad he hadn't been able to break the news to Cora. He drew up short on the boardwalk. If they hadn't been interrupted, that girl might have a home right now. "Holly."

She didn't answer. Probably couldn't hear him. She was mesmerized by the Christmas tree on display behind the glass. This was the third time she had fallen behind. He knew why. She was dreaming about Christmas at her new home with her ma, wishing and praying with all her might.

He waited, keeping a careful eye out. Something didn't feel right. He couldn't put his finger on what, so he stayed attentive. The door to the dry-goods store swung open and a severe-looking woman with a raised broom headed straight for Holly.

"Shoo! Get away from my window! Your kind isn't welcome here!"

He stood in front of Holly. "Calm down, ma'am. She isn't doing any harm."

"She's scaring away customers." The woman rounded on him with the vigor of a feral cat. "And I just washed that glass. And you… I'm calling the sheriff, that's what I'll do!"

"Don't you hurt that child, ma'am," he said, while Holly stared, confused. Poor thing. "Come, Holly. Let's move along."

"Riffraff!" the woman said.

He had been called worse. He kept a hand on Holly's shoulder, moving her along. He didn't bother to hurry. The woman didn't concern him much. He could feel her disdain pouring after him like a chill on the wind. He was used to it. Some people considered him no better than an outlaw, never mind that his work made their world safer.

"That's what Mrs. Beams called me." Holly's hand crept into his and held on tightly.

"Don't you pay any mind to folk like that. They have their own set of problems."

"I was just lookin'." She sighed, dragging her feet at the next window display. "That one's got a real doll. Not a corncob, but a real doll."

"Now, I can't afford a fancy porcelain doll." He meant to sound gruff, but it didn't come out that way.

The girl sighed again. "I was just lookin', is all."

Maybe he would have to come back and buy that doll, maybe when he stopped by the sheriff's to make sure the charges were going to stick. It wouldn't hurt the girl to have a nice Christmas present.

They cut down the alley and took the back way into the hotel. The stairs creaked and the place was drafty, but after he got a fire built in the stoves in both rooms, it was comfortable. While Holly laid out her new purchases on her bed and told her doll all about them, he sat down with the gold-and-pearl-inlaid sewing case.

Cora Emmaline Bauer Sims was etched in fancy lettering across the top.

Cora Emmaline Bauer Sims, according to the land office, owned her shop and her house outright. He opened the delicate case and ran a callused fingertip over the fine velvet-and-silk lining. All the utensils were missing, places where a thimble, scissors, needles and various other sewing tools had once neatly fit. It was a wonder that Holly had been able to hold on to it.

The memory of Cora's pretty blush stayed with him. In his mind's eye he could see her lovely face pinkening and her eyes deepening to a captivating blue. He went to put away the sewing kit and caught his reflection in the bureau mirror. Gruff. Rugged. A loaded gun at either hip.

Too bad he didn't have a chance with her. He frowned at his reflection. He was no prize. No fine lady wanted a man who made a living with his gun. He was a loner; being alone was what he knew. It was safer.

She sure was nice, though. Peace filled him as he remembered their talk. He'd never known the simple pleasure of sitting and talking with a lady. It surprised him how much he liked listening to her and seeing more of who she was. She had been able to tease out pieces of his life story, too, something he never told anyone.

"Mr. Rafe?" Holly padded in with her corncob doll cradled in the crook of her arm. "Did you find her yet?"

He steeled up all the weakened places so that not a single feeling leaked out. "Remember what I told you?"

"I know." She sighed, running a finger down the

handkerchief she'd borrowed to wrap like a dress around the dried corncob. She fussed with the fabric as if she carried a precious china doll. "I gotta wait. You can find her, right?"

"I'm doing my best, Holly. You have to trust me."

"But what if she ain't here? What if she died?" She hugged her doll gently, the way a good mother would. A tear dripped onto the doll's dress. "If she's dead, you ain't gonna find her."

"She's not dead." He felt like a donkey's behind. "I don't want you worrying."

"Then why haven't you found her?"

"I'm working on it. You leave it to me. I'm good at what I do, I promise you that." He wanted to tell Holly that her ma had been the woman who'd waited on her today, but how could he? He guessed Cora had been brutally taken advantage of in her past. How would she take this news? Some women were forever broken by a terrible crime like that. He figured others found a way to bury the memory and piece their lives together the best they could, which was sort of how he had managed to move on from the war.

Cora had made a nice life for herself in this town. That told him she was a strong woman. But strong enough to face the child she'd worked so hard to forget? The one irrefutable reminder of a crime? He didn't know the answer to that.

"Mr. Rafe? I like all my new things. Miss Cora was awful nice to me." Holly kept hugging her doll, looking small and uncertain and alone.

He surely knew how that felt. Seeing her reminded

him of being a boy, aching for a mother's love and a father's attention and knowing it could never be. Not even when he had been with the Tildens. They had been kind to him, but it wasn't the same. They knew they were always going to send him on and there was no attachment, no caring. Loneliness gnawed at him like a hungry wolf. He shook his head, annoyed at himself. What had happened to his self-control? Wasn't he going to stay detached? Uninvolved?

"I'm glad you're happy, Holly." He cleared his throat, doing his best to sound curt. "We want you to look nice when you meet your ma."

"Do you reckon she'll like me?"

He did his best, but those big blue eyes did him in. He wasn't man enough to fight it, not anymore. He cared about the girl. He cared what happened to her more than he should. More than what was smart.

"I reckon she will." He remembered the image of Cora showing a green dress to Holly—he'd been keeping watch from the shop across the street. He cleared his throat, uneasy with the feelings stirring within him. He had no business caring about someone else. It wasn't as if he knew anything about being a father. "Go to bed. It's late."

"Yessir!" She scampered off, clutching her doll, leaving him alone in his room. She'd left the door half-open, and he could see her kneeling at the foot of her bed. He had never met anyone so full of prayers.

He hoped God really could hear the lonely wishes of an orphan. Because he hoped that Cora would want her child now that time had passed and she'd had a chance to heal. That was the outcome he sure hoped for, the happy ending he would pray for, if he could.

If only he could get rid of the tight feeling dead center in his chest and the punch of alarm in his gut. He feared trouble was ahead and he could do nothing to stop it. Not one blessed thing.

Chapter Six

Rafe Jones. He was all Cora could think about even two days later. As she sat in church waiting for him and Holly to arrive, her thoughts were still on him as they had been every moment since they had last parted. Yesterday throughout her workday, her gaze had gone to the front windows to keep watch for a certain dark-coated stranger. Every stitch she made on one of Holly's dresses by evening reminded her of sitting in her back room, listening to him speak. She could hear the deep rich timbre of his voice and his heart in his words.

This morning had been no different. She shifted on the church pew to get a better look at the open door. Cold wind and meager sunshine poured in as the faithful shivered into the vestibule and down the main aisle.

"Miss Sims." Rhett Jorgenson tipped his hat and stopped, a surprise since he had always kept a deliberate distance between them. He towered over her, dashing as always, but now his handsome forehead was pinched and his rugged good looks darkened. "I need to know about that bounty hunter I saw hanging around your store. He's not giving you any trouble?"

"Goodness, no." Not to be rude, but she glanced at the back again. She did not want to miss Rafe and Holly. "I'm sewing a new wardrobe for Mr. Jones's young ward."

"Oh, so he's a customer."

How strange. Mr. Jorgenson had never been curious about her customers before. "If he's in need of new boots, I'll be sure to recommend you."

"I appreciate that." The merchant hesitated. Strange how he stood there, seeming uncertain. Uncertain was not Rhett Jorgenson's style. "I heard you were robbed. Are you sure it has nothing to do with this rough? He's a gunman, the best in the territory, according to Dobbs. Those types of men are untrustworthy. You're a God-fearing woman. You don't understand the way the world works."

"Oh, I understand just fine." For all the bachelor's good looks, Cora saw something else now. She did not find him interesting in the least. "Good day to you."

A familiar family crowded into the sanctuary. Joanna McKaslin, her husband and their two children. Her friend spotted her and gave a friendly wave before following her husband to their usual pew near the back.

"Cora?" A woman's voice had her whipping around. Lu Evans, who owned the town bakery, had crept down the aisle in front and was peering at her over the back of the bench. "Do you know what I have been hearing?"

"That my special Christmas rates at the shop are extended until Christmas Eve?"

"Oh, you stop teasing," Lu said with mirth. "You know good and well what I am talking about. A certain rugged bounty hunter dined with you with the other night. *And* he has been spotted at your shop a couple of times."

"I'm pleading the Fifth."

"That says it all, honey. I'll keep hoping. Love can come into a woman's life at any time. I met my Harvey when I was thirty-one. Now we're an old married couple with our children grown and gone. There's no reason that can't happen to you."

Those were exactly the words she had been too afraid to think. So much could go wrong on this perilous journey from meeting to courting to marriage. Romance had never worked for her. Men had never seen her as more than passable. Until Rafe. When he spoke to her, it was as if the entire world melted away. When he listened to her, he seemed to pay attention with his entire being. His caring regard made her soul sparkle like a candlelit Christmas tree.

Suddenly a silence swept through the sanctuary. She twisted in her seat, her eyes meeting his instantly. He stood several inches above all the other men. He looked rugged, yes, but tame. As they shared a long-distance smile, joy came to her heart.

The child at his side waved and hauled him through the crowd and down the aisle. She was adorable in the green wool dress and matching bonnet. In his usual black, Rafe seemed to draw all the attention as he stalked down the aisle. With every step closer, the sugar-cookie warmth of the connection they had shared returned and grew stronger.

"I'm so glad you've come." Cora slid down the pew to make room for them. "Holly, you look very pretty."

"You ain't just sayin' that?"

"Not even a little bit."

Surprise and disbelief marked the girl's face. "Pa used to say that, but…" She fell silent and let out a wobbly breath as if some things were too painful to say aloud. "I love the dress sooo much. Thank you, Miss Cora."

"My pleasure, dear girl." She couldn't help the tug of affection for the orphan. Her twin braids were far from even. Clearly someone with no experience had plaited her hair. There was time to fix that before the service began. Lu had not started playing the organ to welcome the worshipers yet. "Would you like me to rebraid your hair?"

"Oh, yes!" Holly clasped her hands together, giving a glimpse of her bright spirit.

"That's kind of you, Cora." Rafe shrugged sheepishly. "Braiding isn't one of my strong suits."

"You did fairly well for a bounty hunter." She dug inside her reticule for her comb.

Feeling his gaze, she turned her attention to the work of untying Holly's braids, but she could not stop her awareness of him. He radiated quiet dignity. It was impossible not to admire him.

"I hope you don't feel too uncomfortable here. You mentioned you were not a churchgoing man."

"I'm not. There's never been anything in my life that would make me want to believe." His jaw muscles went tight and he shrugged out of his overcoat. He watched her work, his emotions unreadable. "I stopped by the sheriff's office. The lowlife I caught with your reticule is named Sol Krantz. He's locked up, trying to make bail."

"That's good. I feel better knowing he's behind bars." She quickly parted and separated fine strands of hair and began plaiting. Rafe's expression sharpened like a dagger.

"Did Krantz threaten you?" His growl was low and dangerous, but she was not afraid.

He was a protective man, that was all. There was nothing dangerous about Rafe Jones. Aware of the child listening, she kept her voice light. "He cautioned me. It's nothing to fret about."

"I say it is. If he talks to you, I want to know about it."

Did he have any notion how wonderful his words sounded to her? She was used to being alone. For a decade she had managed her own business, owned her own home and been the sole provider and parent for her two nephews. Every problem, every shortfall and every hardship over those years she had shouldered on her own. For the first time in her adult life, she was not alone.

She tied a ribbon onto the end of the first braid and started another. The organ began to play an aching rendition of "Amazing Grace." The gentle notes rose above the rustling of fidgety children and subdued conversations. "How is the search for Holly's mother going?"

"Well." That was it, just one word. That was all he was going to reveal.

She peered through her lashes at him while she worked the second braid. He watched her as if he admired what he saw.

He could be the one. He could be the man for her. The one who would change her life with his love. The one who would hold her close, the man she could trust with all her heart and soul. As she tied off the braid and fussed with the ribbon, she considered what little she knew about him. He was a mystery. What she did know about him broke her heart. He had been an orphan. He'd served in the war. He was a man without home or anyone to care about him. He was a bounty hunter who had let an orphaned girl hire him for a few pennies. Didn't that say something remarkable about him? Perhaps that was all she really needed to know.

The hymn's melody reminded her that everyone was lost, that everyone was given a second chance. Maybe the man all in black, who had no reason to believe in anything, had been brought here for a reason.

"Miss Cora?" Holly scooted into place against the pew's back. "Thank you lots. I sure like my hair. You tie a real good bow. This was my pa's favorite song."

"It's one of mine, too." She smiled over the girl's head at the solemn man, sitting so still and shadowed. Tenderness sifted through her. She adored him. This was no fantasy, no wishful thinking or dream. The affection she felt for him—from him—was as real as the stone floor beneath her feet.

For the first time she could see clearly. Rafe Jones

was a divine blessing that had come into her life like the first snow of the Christmas season.

She was not unwanted, after all.

"How would you like to accompany us to dinner over at the hotel?" Rafe said to Cora as he took Cora's hand, so small in his own, to help her over a patch of ice. The connection hit him like a mallet; it was more emotion than he felt comfortable with. He steadied himself. He could face down some of the most treacherous outlaws without one lick of fear. Why couldn't he do the same with Cora?

"I would like to accept."

She had that "uh-oh" look on her pretty face. That told him he was out of luck. Disappointment washed through him. "A lovely lady like yourself probably has a better invitation, I reckon."

Plenty of dapper, professional, acceptable types lived in this town. Maybe one of them had asked her when he hadn't been looking.

"No, I meant that I had other plans for you." She smiled at him.

Why her smile drove every thought from his head, he couldn't say.

"What plans?" Holly, who had been skipping ahead of them, wanted to know. "Miss Cora, do I getta come, too?"

"Of course." She turned pink with joy.

She sure was a lovely sight. He could look at her all the day long and never grow tired. Maybe it was being inside that church, sitting there like anyone else, that had made him realize he was hoping. For what? What were the chances a lady like Cora would accept a man like him?

None, that was what. So why was he hoping there might be? It was how she treated him, like a man of worth. How her friends and family had greeted him with genuine welcome after the service.

"I made stew and corn bread last night, hoping the two of you might want to dine with me." Cora's voice was like music, soft and light. It went up and down like a song. "Does that sound good to you?"

"Yep! I love corn bread. I ain't had some in so long." Holly clung to Cora's hand. "Mr. Rafe, don't you want corn bread, too?"

"You know I do."

"Hurray!" Holly leaped in place. "Do you got your own house, Miss Cora?"

"I do." It was hard, Cora thought, not to be even more charmed by the child. It took so little to please her, and the Sunday service had lifted her spirits. Cora gave thanks for that. With all the child had been through, she deserved to have her mother found and a good life ahead of her, God willing. "I have one of your dresses almost finished. You can take a look at it and give me your opinion."

"Okay." The girl clung to her more tightly. "Do you reckon my ma can sew?"

"Most women can." She did not add that there was a very good chance she knew Holly's mother if she was indeed a resident of the town. Most women came to her shop for a special occasion like a wedding or baptism if they could not afford to hire a seamstress.

"Enough about your ma." Rafe sounded curt, but the corners of his mouth were turned up in a smile. "You'll talk Cora's ears off the way you've done mine."

"I reckon so." Holly sighed, but she did not look overly distraught. Mischief twinkled in her eyes. "Mr. Rafe says I talk enough for three girls. That he's never met anyone as talkative as me."

"I wouldn't trust Mr. Rafe's opinion overly much." It was so easy to jest when she was happy. She cast a glance at the man beside her and his smile widened. "He might be the best gunman in the territory, but he doesn't know a whole lot about girls."

"He couldn't even braid my hair." Holly was quick to agree. "So maybe I don't talk too much."

"I should think not. I hope you don't mind dessert, because I picked up a chocolate cake at the bakery."

"*Chocolate* cake?" Holly's eyes widened. "I ain't never had that before."

"It's good, trust me." They had turned down her street. In the soft, gray light the tall, leafless trees had a silvered glow. Frost clung to every surface like a glaze, making her modest home inviting.

"Are you sure you want me to come inside?" Rafe leaned close, keeping his voice low. "Your neighbors are staring."

Indeed they were. She cast a look along the street and saw the Nelsons standing on their front porch with frowns on their faces. Across the lane, Mr. Holland had poked his head out of his door, eyes narrowed.

"My reputation has preceded me." He stopped, grimacing.

"I hope it has." She kept going. "Are you coming?"

"I'm considering. Will my being in your house make trouble for you?"

"It's cold out here." She held out her hand. "Come inside and warm up. It will only take me a minute to get the meal on the table."

That was what she said, but he realized her answer was something else, something left unsaid. He was wanted. For the first time. For real. The cold in his heart melted further. She probably had no notion what her acceptance meant to him. Gratitude was *one* emotion, the only one he felt comfortable naming. He took her delicate hand in his, savoring the precious feeling of belonging it brought. Companionship was nice. Acceptance was better.

Holly was sure getting herself a good ma—that was the only way he could think of Cora. Hope nudged at him like a persistent winter wind, trying to blow him off course. What he wanted and what he was going to get were two different things. So different, in fact, it was best not to go wanting at all.

But that was hard to do as Cora unlocked the door to her snug house. He held the door for the girl and woman, bracing himself before following them across the threshold and into the warm and cozy home.

Two sofas flanked a stone hearth, where a potbellied stove sat dark and still. A large window with a built-in window seat offered a pleasant view of the large front yard. Framed daguerreotypes of her nephews at various ages marched along the main wall. On the far wall was a comfortable sewing corner with a sewing machine and a small table heaped with baskets of fabrics, probably works in progress.

Colorful hand-braided rugs made the dark floor cheery. Afghans were hung over the backs of the sofas and the big chair near the window. Snug enough to invite a man to sit down, put up his feet, soak in the aroma of supper cooking and relax for a spell.

"Is this my dress?" Holly had wandered over to peer into the different baskets.

"Two of them, yes. I've only just cut out the red fabric you liked, but the lavender wool, that one is basted. I'll show you after dinner." Cora took Holly's coat and hung it on a peg next to the door.

Rafe shook his head, drawing his thoughts back to the reason he was here. He felt the weight of the delicate sewing case in his coat pocket. What mattered was Holly. She was the reason he was standing in Cora's parlor. He oughtn't to be dreaming for himself. This would be a fine place for the girl. She had a home. She had a mother. She was one child who would not be lost and forgotten by this world. Not now.

The females were leaving him for the kitchen. He could see through the wide doorway to the serviceable, spotless cooking range along the back wall. He imagined it, too, as a pleasant room with a sunny corner for a table and chairs. As he hunkered down in front of the potbellied stove and took the poker to the carefully banked coals, he noticed a closed door tucked off to one side. Probably went upstairs to the bedrooms. He liked to think of Holly having a nice room of her own, with pretty things and that china doll he was going to leave behind for her.

He added coal from the hop and closed the door. Heat built inside as he stood. Voices mumbled pleasantly from the next room. A clank from a cast-iron pot rang out and he couldn't ignore the rich beefy aroma of bubbling stew. A clink and clatter of ironware and steel knives and spoons had him picturing the mother and daughter setting the table together.

Just get it over with, Jones. Tell her. He bent to adjust the damper; the fire was burning just fine. No good was going to come from putting it off a moment longer. They were alone here. No one would come along and interrupt. He ought to just blurt it out and leave. That would be the easy thing for his aching heart.

The right thing was something else entirely. Cora breezed into view with pan in hand. Her dark brown skirts swirled around her ankles as she moved to the cooking range and slipped the corn bread to heat in the oven. She repositioned the pan on the racks, and he appreciated her unconscious grace as she straightened. Tiny wisps curled out of her elegant knot, framing her face like a cloud.

She was everything a man could ever want. Everything a man like him could never dare to dream of. His chest felt heavy and tight, and he seemed too big and rough as she smiled at him with unbridled kindness.

"Oh, you built the fire. Thank you for that. I have some tea steeping, if you would like to come to the table. I don't want you out here alone, Rafe."

It felt as if she was saying something else. It felt as if he was, too. "I'd sure appreciate a cup of tea. It's bitter cold today."

"Only outside." She said nothing more and took his hand, as if she understood perfectly what he was too shy to say.

Chapter Seven

"It's a good life you've made for yourself here, Cora."

At Rafe's compliment, tiny bubbles of joy popped within her. She couldn't remember a more enjoyable afternoon, but she was rapidly learning that any time spent in Rafe's company was better than with anyone else. "A decade ago, I wasn't sure how things would work out when I climbed off the stagecoach. It left me in a cloud of dust, thinking I hope this isn't a big mistake."

"It couldn't have been a wiser choice. It says something about you, how you built all this from a new start."

"Now you're making me seem like something I'm not. I've only done what anyone would do." She plucked the cozy from the teapot and wrapped her fingers around the smooth, ceramic handle. Self-conscious, both with his compliments and his powerful attention, she blushed again as she refilled his cup. "Everyone wants a new start and a happy life."

"Every now and then," he said, "I see someone I track down truly remorseful over what they've done. They are the ones who are living an honest life, trying to make up for things. When I show up, it's a reminder that life has its own justice in the end."

"I believe that."

He captivated her. They had spent the past few hours talking. Being with him was like waking up to an impossibly perfect dream.

She filled her cup and set the pot aside. She hardly was aware of stirring sugar into her tea or the blur of motion outside the window where Holly was swinging on the boys' old wooden swing. "Have you ever longed for a new start?" she asked.

"All the time lately." His gaze speared hers with enough force to make her pulse still.

"L-lately?" Did she dare hope that she was the reason? Her hand shook as she set down the spoon. The amber liquid in her cup swirled like a tornado. That was how she felt inside, all twisting and swirling. "Have you ever wanted to do anything else aside from bounty hunting?"

"I'd be a gunsmith." His answer came without hesitation. "I'd get me a little shop and repair guns."

"I can see you doing that." It was easy to imagine him sitting at work at a table with a rifle in pieces before him. "You would be good at it. But maybe you like being a bounty hunter better?"

"There's nothing to like. It's just what I do." His throat worked as if with emotion, and he glanced out the window at Holly. He cleared his throat. "Truth is, I've never had any cause to settle down anywhere or a reason to stay. Lately I keep wondering what it would be like to have a life like yours. With friends and church and family."

Her heart stopped. "I have a nice life, but it has been…lonely."

"Lonely. I know what that is." He swallowed hard, as if trying even harder to keep his emotions down. "Everywhere you look, no one seems right for you. You've got no family. No roots. Nothing, so you've got to make it on your own."

"Yes. That's it exactly."

"After the workday is done and the supper dishes are put away," he said, "there's a long stretch of lonely gnawing at you. You don't notice it so much when you're busy, but when you're still, it hurts like a bullet wound."

She never realized all they had in common. They were more alike than different. He understood her, at heart. Affection for him sang through her like a hymn, pure and powerful, resonating in her soul.

"Yes," she said. "All the years that pass and the people you meet, something is always missing. You look around and others seem to have found it. While you're happy for them, you measure time by days passing, instead of anniversaries and a child's birth and every change as he or she grows. Your life stays as if in shadow even as you long for the light."

"And then someone comes along and everything is different. Changed." He stood, moving from his chair across the table to Holly's empty chair, next to Cora. He was so close she could see the rough texture of his unshaven jaw, notice the darker flecks of obsidian in his storm-gray eyes and feel the radiant caring of his big heart.

Changed. That was what he had done. She was different and brimming with hope because of him. As he thoughtfully gathered her hands in his with infinite care, love claimed her heart. Not in a giddy rush or with a sudden proclamation as she always thought it would, but in a quiet, calm whisper like dawn's first light in midwinter. Gentle and sure and bringing light to shadowed, forgotten places. Love so bright it ached deeper and deeper within her, bringing tears to her eyes.

Her vision may have been blurred, but she could feel his caring. Never had any man looked at her with such tender adoration, as if her feelings mattered most to him, as if she was most precious to him.

Love lingered silently between them, unbroken by the roar of the fire in the stove and the faint tick of the clock on the wall. Time passed—she did not know how much. With every breath she took, bliss filled her. This man's love—his tenderness, his respect, his devotion—was all she wanted.

Gratitude came from the bottom of her soul. Rafe loved her. She could see it, she could feel it. He made all the emptiness within her vanish.

"There's something I have to ask you, Cora."

"Y-yes?"

"I don't know how to do this." He grew serious and as still as a statue. "I've never done anything like this before."

"Y-you haven't?" She watched him hopefully.

"Nope. I'm not good with words. Terrible when it comes to personal things. What I am good with is a gun, but that won't help me here."

"Then I will be very understanding and patient while you figure it out."

"That may take a spell." He hesitated, wrestling with the words he had been practicing late last night. Her smile could change a man like him. Her calm joy made him want to be with her forever. How was he going to stand bringing up her past? He couldn't stomach it. He was going to hurt her. Some things in the past were best left there. He truly believed that.

Somehow he had to make this right for her. He took a gulp of air and thought of the peace he had sensed in the church today. He wished that peace for her now.

"I want to show you something." Maybe he'd do best giving her the sewing box. He gently released her hands and circled around to his chair. His duster jacket was hung up neatly over the back of his chair. Pulse racing, he lifted the slim case from the pocket and held it out for her to see.

"That can't be." She went pale. "However did you find this?"

"Was it yours?" He returned to her side, hating the way the sound of his boot heels was like a death knell. He hated being the bearer of difficult news. But surely, this would be all right in the end. That thought sustained him as he set the case on the table.

"Yes. My grandmother gave it to me on my seventh birthday. She said I was old enough to learn to sew." Tears stood in her eyes. Her slender fingers brushed the top of the case, lovingly touching the letters of her name. "I was named after her. She was a wonderful woman and I still miss her."

"You have had a lot of loss in your life."

"You've had loss, too, but of a different sort."

"It's more like what I haven't found." Until now. Part of him was ready to admit that he was more than fond of her. He was more than sweet on her. He was walking on dangerous ground.

"I don't understand. Did you find this here in town?"

"No." Steeling himself, holding back every ounce of feeling, he concentrated on the child outside. "That case is why I came to town."

"I don't understand."

"Holly had it. It was a keepsake kept by her pa to remind her of her mother. Apparently Holly's mother left her as a baby. I don't think the pa was the real father. It looks as if she was adopted."

"I still don't understand. You came to town to bring this to me?"

"No, Cora. I came to town to bring Holly to you. To her mother."

No man had ever spoken to her with as much tender caring. He gathered her hands in his again. "I know only a terrible tragedy could have made you leave a newborn, but Holly has no one else. There are no living relatives. I found a few of the father's parishioners, who said there was no other family. The territory wasn't very settled ten years ago. There are no records, no letters, no papers, not even one for the adoption. I'm sorry to bring up this pain, but—"

"It was you." She didn't mean to interrupt him, but the words just popped out. "I felt watched the day I was robbed. You were the one watching me. That's how you saw the robbery. It was you."

"Guilty." He winced but didn't look sorry. "I had to see what sort of woman you were. If you were kind, or no better than the woman I found Holly with. That's all. I didn't mean any disrespect."

"And so you were trying to get to know me." All of his questions. All of their quite personal conversations. Understanding hammered through her. He had not been interested in her romantically. He had not been falling in love with her. Of course not. He would never be captivated by a plain brown bird like her. What had she been thinking?

Disappointment struck like a blow. Reeling from the impact, she tore her hands from his and bounded out of her chair. With every breath she took, she could feel her heart breaking. How had she let herself believe? All these years no man had ever been swept away by her. How could she have been so foolish?

"Cora." No man could be more compassionate. He ambled toward her. "I know this comes as a surprise to you. I had to look out for Holly's welfare. She hired me to."

"With three pennies." That made him perfect in her estimation. She swiped at her eyes, hating the tears that blurred her view of him and betrayed her emotions. She blinked hard, willing her vision to clear. Any moment, he would guess at her misplaced love for him. How pathetic she was going to look when he realized that she thought he was about to proclaim his intentions for marriage.

Pain crackled like winter lightning through her. He was talking, and she tried to calm her emotions to hear what he was saying. Something about how sorry he was for what happened to her. It was the agony on his face that shocked her the most. He was a good, caring man, which was what had confused her. Here he was concerned about a violent crime against her that had never happened. He was anguished by the thought of her having been harmed.

It was time to spare them both more agony. She wiped the tears from her cheeks and dug deep for the right words. "Rafe, you have mistaken me for someone else."

"No, I am very sure. I telegraphed every major town in the territory. You are the only Cora Sims. There is no other."

"Yes, but I have never had a child." Looking at his sincere confusion only made her heart break even more. She loved this man. She feared she always would. Drawing in a shaky breath, she faced him. Let him look in her eyes and see the truth. "I'm truly not Holly's mother."

"But she has your sewing kit, Cora. You admitted it was yours."

"Once, long ago, yes."

"Then I'm asking you to accept Holly." He rubbed away more tears on her cheeks with the pads of his thumbs.

Those stubborn tears. She blinked harder, but more

of them fell. She didn't know if she was crying for Holly or for herself. "My sewing kit was sold along with everything of value after my father died. I haven't seen this since I was eleven."

"But—" he finally seemed to be hearing her "—if you didn't leave it with her as a baby, then…"

"I don't know. Somehow it must have found its way to Holly's family." She longed for him to take her hands in his again and to feel his solid comfort. Pain twisted through her for Holly, for him and for the love she would never have. "I've never had a child and no tragic attack that could have given me one. I'm sorry, Rafe."

"Then you're not her ma." Devastation carved into his features.

"No, although I wish I was." She watched the girl outside, gaining confidence on the swing and gliding higher. Snow fell like pieces of dreams. The wind gusted again, signaling the coming storm. The girl had to be getting cold, and yet she looked happy as she swung toward the sky and fell back to earth again. "What will become of her now?"

"Don't know." His voice was strained and uneven, gruff, not with anger but defeat. "I thought for sure—" He didn't finish, staring, instead, out the window at the child who played innocently unaware that she had lost her only real hope for a mother and for a home. "I don't have any other leads. There simply are none."

"If there is something I can do, some way I can help you search, I would be happy to. I'm excellent at writing letters."

"You have to understand, Cora, there is no one. The

orphanage she'd been with had a fire and the records were lost. Holly's pa moved to Montana Territory from back East, but no one knew where. You were Holly's last chance."

"Her last chance? Me?" Rafe saw tears silver her eyes. "That's breaking me."

"Me, too." His jaw worked. It was tough keeping so much dammed up inside. He couldn't believe it. He was good at his job. He had a knack for following leads and hunting down impossible cases. Never had he been so wrong. He grabbed the case from the table, turning it over in his hands. He had been so sure. "What am I going to do? What is *she* going to do?"

"You aren't going to take her back to an orphanage, are you?"

Outside, the little girl noticed they were looking her way and smiled widely. She was a different girl from the one who had come up to him on that Helena street. Gone were the patched hand-me-downs and the hungry eyes, replaced by a healthy complexion and hope. How was he going to take that away? He hid the case in his pocket, safely out of sight. "What choice do I have?"

"I don't know. How hard is it to find a good home for a child?"

"Nearly impossible is my guess." Why else would there be so many unwanted orphans? He knew that for a fact. "I can't believe this. I failed her."

The only one who had ever relied on him, and he'd failed her. Defeat became too big to describe. It suffocated him with a mix of regret and self-recrimination. He couldn't bear the thought of what he had done.

"She doesn't know?" Cora's question was tremulous, as if she felt crushed, too.

"No. She can't read. She doesn't know a single letter. She's kept that case all this time. Either no one read the name for her or no one knew about it. She says her pa bought it for her ma." Second- or thirdhand. He hadn't considered that before. It wasn't like him not to consider every angle. Maybe there was a bigger truth at work. Something beyond his need to find a mother for Holly. The first time he had spotted Cora Sims closing up her dress shop, rational thought had fled his mind, leaving insanity in its place.

Insane. Yep, that sounded about right. Because he had to be insane to start imagining life in a town like this, in a house like this, with a woman like Cora. He didn't belong here or anywhere. He was as homeless as Holly and twice as unwanted.

Best to face that fact and not let it bother him. Feelings did no good for a man like him. "There is a small blessing in all this. I'm glad nothing bad happened to you, Cora."

"Rafe, I—" She stopped.

That got him to wondering what she'd been about to say. Something bonded them, he couldn't deny that. He would give anything for that bond to turn into more.

The door banged open and Holly came in, dappled with snow, her cheeks rosy with happiness. She looked as if she belonged in this tidy kitchen with the lace curtains and ruffled chair cushions. It about shattered him to think she wouldn't be growing up in this safe home with cake on a plate on the counter and Cora as her ma. That was the life this nice girl deserved, not the one she had waiting for her.

He thought of that Beams woman and shivered. Holly was not going back there. That left an orphanage or someone looking for a child to take for work exchange. The thought of her laboring on a farm somewhere for food in her belly—no. Fierce anger thundered through him. It wasn't going to happen. What was the alternative? Was there one? It wasn't as if he could keep her, hauling her with him as he tracked down dangerous men.

"I'm frozen up like an icicle." Holly trudged deeper into the kitchen. Snow tracked behind her, marring the polished floor.

Cora didn't react, not to the snow, anyway. That didn't surprise him, but it did strengthen his resolve. She was the kindest woman he had ever known. He more than liked her. He adored her. Somehow he was going to have to face that.

"Come right here and stand in front of the stove." Loving goodness, that was Cora. He saw her more clearly than ever as she guided the child by the shoulders. "I'll get you a cookie to nibble on while you warm up."

"Thank you, Miss Cora." Holly beamed up at the woman in sheer adoration.

"We had best take that cookie with us, kid," he said. "We've got to get back to the hotel."

"We do? Can't we stay here longer, Mr. Rafe? I like it here." There was a bigger question in the girl's eyes, one of bare hope. He feared she knew why they had been spending so much time with Cora, and that was why her lower lip wobbled.

He hadn't been so smart, after all. He felt like dirt. No, he felt lower than dirt. He grabbed his coat, fighting a strange lump in his throat. "We'd best go, Holly. Cora, thanks for having us to dinner."

"It was my pleasure." Tears stood in her eyes, in her luminous eyes full of love.

He had never beheld a greater beauty. No one had ever looked at him that way. In a blink, that honesty had faded, but the feelings remained. How could one look jolt him like an earthquake? How could one fine woman feel that for him? His boots became steel, too heavy to lift. Maybe the truth was tougher. He didn't want to walk away. He wished to heaven today had gone differently. That Holly would have had a ma to love her and he would have—

No, there was no point in wishing. He shrugged into his coat, fighting to keep emotion from his voice, but that lump remained in his throat, betraying him. "Let's get going, Holly."

"Yes, sir."

Cora watched him with tears in her eyes, unshed and aching with pain.

Yep, he thought as he closed the door. He felt the same way. There was no happy ending here. He led the way through the snow falling like those wintry pieces of his heart.

Chapter Eight

They had left, the big man and the small girl who had stolen her heart, walking down the pathway side by side. Cora dropped onto the window seat, hollow, shivering despite the roaring fire in the stove. Iciness crept in through the glass, seeping into her very soul. Hot, unfallen tears pooled, making the vision of the man and child blur. They were her dream, gone forever now. Rafe had never loved her. And Holly, that poor girl. What would become of her?

She swiped at her face, hating that her fingers came away wet. She was not crying for herself. Her heart was destroyed, but she had done it to herself. That was what came when a woman like her set her hopes too high. They were bound to be dashed. She knew better. What made sobs tear out of her was the thought of a child alone, completely, without a safe home and the chance to go to school. Books lined the shelf next to the door, packed with wonderful stories. Holly would never know the pleasure of being carried away to Dickens's England or meeting Austen's Bennet sisters or Brontë's haunting moors.

She would never play with friends in her yard, go sledding down the street or run screaming over a game of tag. She would never know the security of having a mother's love, someone to braid her hair and sew pretty dresses and help soothe her childhood dilemmas with cookies and kindness.

Cora leaned her forehead against the glass, miserable for the lost child. Holly was nothing more than a gray shadow now, veiled by snowfall, trudging away with her hand tucked in Rafe's. Her head was bowed forward, as if she was crying. The man and child took another step and the haze of snow enveloped them, stealing them forever from her sight.

Please watch over them, Lord. I know You have a plan, but it is hard to see.

She had never felt so bleak. A knock on the back door rang like a gunshot through the silent house. She started, then pushed away from the glass with the wild hope that Rafe and Holly had come back. She was halfway to the kitchen when she realized that of course they hadn't, and certainly not to the back door. Emmett strode in, key in hand, flecked with snow and grinning ear to ear.

"I was hopin' you would feed me." He was unashamed of his shameless self-invitation, bless him.

"The stew is still warm and I have cake." She blinked away the last of her tears, glad none were on her face, and forced what she hoped would pass for a smile. "Let me take your coat. You are a welcome sight, dear boy."

"You are, too." He shrugged out of his jacket and unwound the scarf from his neck. She had made both for him. How handsome he looked, so strapping and grown up as he kissed her cheek. "I got to missing you."

"Me? What on earth is there to miss about me?" Although she was pleased as she hung up his things. She scurried to the stove to pour him a bracing cup of tea. "I would have thought you were doing something much more interesting than sitting in your spinster aunt's kitchen."

"I'm not courting any young lady in town, so where else would I be?"

Apparently not in the place he rented above the hardware store. She set the tea on the table, determined not to hint about a certain young lady in town he might want to get to know. He might not admit he was interested, but Cora knew her nephew. Down deep he was bashful. He took time getting to know people. As she dished up a bowl of stew, she remembered the timid boy who had climbed off the stagecoach, leading his younger brother. Emmett had been a bit older than Holly, with wide, sad eyes.

"You spoil me, Aunt Cora." Emmett eagerly took the bowl from her and finished serving himself. "You stop waiting on me, you hear? You've done your duty. I'm all grown up."

"Nonsense. You know how I love to fuss." That was what she called it, but it was more than that. Taking care of her nephews was a joy and a privilege, and she sorely missed it. "I need to get in all the fussing I can, because soon you will be leading your own life, as you ought to be. So indulge me."

"All right, but I fully intend to fill your coal boxes and shovel your walk before I leave." He took his bowl to the table and dug into the stew. "Want to tell me what's going on with that Jones fellow?"

Pain rasped through her. Refusing to let it show, she drew in a breath, straightened her shoulders and took a sip of tea, now cold. She had forgotten to refill her cup. She was more distraught over Rafe than she cared to admit. She had fallen for a man who had not fallen for her. "He's bought several dresses for his young ward. I suppose we are acquaintances of sorts. We have some things in common, since I understand how challenging it is to suddenly find yourself raising a child."

"Oh, I think it's more than that. A man like Jones doesn't sit with a lady in church because the two of them are 'acquaintances.'"

"What do you mean?" She had misinterpreted Rafe's interest in her. That was a fact. Now that it was proved she was not Holly's mother, why would she see Rafe for any reason outside of her work?

"I asked around. I wanted to know more about this Mr. Jones." Emmett stirred sugar into his tea. "One of the deputies said he's no man to mess with. He's smart, fair and honest and the best gunman anyone has ever seen in these parts. He always gets his man. He brought in the notorious Clarkston Crow without a scratch, after two marshals and four bounty hunters died in earlier attempts."

"Goodness." She remembered the capture of the notorious outlaw. It had been in the newspaper two years ago. Crow had not left anyone alive who could identify him when he robbed banks, trains or stagecoaches. For a good part of that year, she knew many people who had been too afraid to travel out of town. "Mr. Jones is quite an impressive man."

"I like him. I like the respect he shows you, Aunt Cora."

"He has been a fine gentleman." It took all her strength to hide her broken feelings. "He rescued Holly from a sad life. Only a truly decent man would do that."

Rafe was a lawman in the most demanding way. He was not tucked safely behind a desk, but risked his life to bring in the bad guy. Her estimation of him remained high. Now, if only she could figure out a way to make her heart stop loving him. She took another sip of cold tea, fighting terrible sadness.

"That was mighty good, Aunt Cora." Emmett set down his spoon with a clatter and shoved back his chair with a loud scrape. Suddenly her home no longer felt so empty and desolate. "Now, where do you want your Christmas tree? You best go clear a place. I've got a spruce in my sleigh. I'll go bring it in."

"You dear boy. Thank you for remembering." She had momentarily forgotten that Christmas was marching closer. It was the time of year meant to remind us of the power of kindness and the saving grace of love. "This blessed season simply isn't the same this time without you boys living here with me."

"You mean dragging in snow on our boots and badgering you about what we're getting for Christmas and searching the house when you're not home trying to find the presents you hid?"

"Yes, that's exactly what I miss. The excitement of having you boys help me decorate cookies and string popcorn. Those were good times. I'm glad I have them to remember."

"Me, too." Emmett grabbed her cup and took it to the counter, then took a fresh one from the cupboard. "You know how much Eli and I appreciate your taking us in. I figured out the other day that I'm older now than you were when we landed on your doorstep."

"It was a big responsibility, but I haven't regretted it for one moment."

"You did a lot for us, Aunt Cora." He poured tea, growing serious. "It was a sacrifice."

"That's part of love." She thought of Rafe and Holly. Had they reached the hotel? Were they packing to leave? Surely they would not leave in a snowstorm. She prayed they would at least say goodbye.

Tears welled in her soul where she hid them, not knowing what else to do. Her heart might be in shreds, but the love she felt for Rafe Jones was whole.

"Are you sure you're all right?" Emmett set the steaming cup on the table in front of her.

"I will be." Thank God for the blessing of this boy, for both her nephews.

"Then you sit and relax while I bring in the tree. Eli will be by shortly. We can all decorate the tree together."

Their walk back to the hotel started out in silence. What was there to say? The snow fell with a vengeance, pummeling them as they went, the wind gusting as if to drive them back to the safety of Cora's home and back to the illusion that Holly belonged to her.

There was no going back, only forward. He did his best to ignore the sniffles Holly tried to hide. He asked her once if she was all right. Her mumbled "Yes, Mr. Rafe" blew away on the cruel wind. Her grip on his hand was tight enough to break bone.

They walked through residential streets where kids were out playing despite the weather. Cheerful screams were muffled by the thick downfall as children made snowmen in one yard or raced down the lane pulling sleds.

Warm windows decked with evergreen boughs gave homey views of garland-crested mantels, of trees lit with tiny candles and of families gathered together. Rafe remembered how it felt inside Cora's house, painstakingly decorated and filled with years of love.

In these houses on tree-lined streets he could see what life might be like. If he yearned for a home and his spirit for shelter where he was wanted, accepted and loved, he kept on walking, aware that Holly did not glance at the playing children or the snug houses. He knew it was easier not to think of what you could never have.

Fury beat through him with a cold fist. It wasn't fair. The girl deserved better. She was a nice little thing. He had to admit he'd grown fond of her. The trouble was, she deserved better than he could give her. What did that leave? Turmoil roiled through him. He had no answers.

The neat rows of houses gave way to the dark

windows of businesses, closed for the day. Snow accumulated on streets and boardwalks, windowsills and rooftops. Silently, as if they were the only two people in town, they passed trees bedecked with ropes of red beads and colorful glass ornaments, safe behind glass. They passed displays of toy trains and dolls with silk dresses and velvet hats, and a single display of a manger, where a newborn was greeted by a donkey and lamb.

"I've been praying and *praying* for the angels to help me." Holly stared hard at the nativity scene. "No matter what, I didn't stop. My pa said you gotta pray with all your heart. You gotta believe. You can't give up no matter what, cuz God is always gonna listen. But I can't remember what my pa looks like no more."

"I wouldn't worry about it if I were you." Comforting a child was nothing he knew. He knelt down, bowed by the desolation on her face. He had never seen such tragic eyes. He brushed snow off her face. "Wherever your pa is, I'm sure he remembers you."

"I surely miss him." Holly's lower lip trembled. "He used to say we didn't have much, but we got what mattered. He said we had love and we had God. But I don't got that no more. Cora ain't my ma, is she?"

"No, I'm sorry. I sure wish she was." Tears fell on her cheeks and he brushed those away, too. "I should have known you'd figure out why we were spending so much time with her."

"I really l-liked her. She's just what I prayed for. I shoulda known it was too good to be true." She trembled, as if with cold, but he sensed the cause was deeper. "We been walkin' all this time and you know what? I tried and tried but I can't pray no more. It's broke inside."

He hated those tears. He hated feeling helpless to fix what was hurting her. "I don't know how, but I'm gonna find you someone nice to take you in."

"There ain't no one. The missus always used to say I got what I deserved. That I was only good for work and I wasn't much good at that. She said don't nobody want me, anyway." Holly's chin lifted, as if she was gathering her strength. "You oughtta take me back, Mr. Rafe. I don't mind so much now."

"What if I mind? I don't want to take you back to that Beams woman."

"I don't have nowhere else to go."

When he looked in her eyes, he saw desolation, the depth and breadth of which he had known himself. He had always known. There was nothing worse in this world than being unwanted. Than being without ties of friends and family, without someone to love and without being loved. It made life a wasteland and made even the best heart wither.

"I know it was a lot to lose. Cora would have made a fine ma." He could see why the girl was broken.

"She's awful k-kind. She said I was p-pretty and she talks to me like I matter." Sobs tore through her like bullets, shaking her hard.

He swept her up and carried her down the block, across the street and into the mean wind. Snow battered them mercilessly as he hiked through town, Holly sobbing all the way. Her pain hurt him worse than anything. It was his fault. He had tried to protect her from this kind of letdown. He'd failed. It just went to show he was no good at raising up a child. Not that he had been considering it, but if he'd wanted to, then it was something best left unconsidered. He would be lousy at it. Holly didn't deserve that, either.

He pushed the back door to the hotel open, taking care not to disturb the girl, who had buried her face in his coat. As he carried her up the stairs, her muffled crying echoed in the stairwell and in the empty places within him. He felt sorely inadequate, as he unlocked the door and laid her on the narrow bed. She clung to him in silent refusal to let go.

Snow was falling off them both. The rooms held a deep chill; he needed to get the fire stoked and the air warmer for her. He couldn't bring himself to break her grip on his coat. She was strong for such a wee thing. How she had any tears left in her, he didn't know. She kept crying, one tear after another with no hope left.

He wished he had some hope to give her. His eyes were smarting. His ice-cold defenses were melting. The gray, wan daylight began to leak from the room as the hours passed. When the girl had finally cried herself to sleep, he spread a blanket over her and went to stir up the embers in the stove.

There was no telling what tomorrow would bring. Most likely they would pack up and head out of town. The thought of leaving Cora brought him to his knees. He sucked in air, doubled over with pain. He used to be a tough bounty hunter, the most feared in three territories. He was surprised to find that at heart he was as vulnerable as any other man. Knotted up with love over the prettiest woman in town and rendered helpless by his duty to a little girl.

It would take a miracle for this to turn out right. He closed the stove, pulled out the damper and, surprising himself, he bowed his head and prayed.

It was late. The boys were gone, leaving behind the memories of their laughter and light teasing, in the way of close brothers everywhere. The house was picked up and the kitchen tidy, the fire roaring in the stove. She was sewing away, and when she was done with work, there was a book waiting for her on the table by the sofa.

Silence echoed around her. She didn't feel as lonely tonight. Her nephews' noisy visit had chased the loneliness from the rooms, but it was more than that. She felt content. She did not feel as if life had passed her by. She had a family who loved her. She had friends she adored. She had her faith, her work, her church work and her lovely home. Blessings surrounded her. She had so much, when others—Rafe and Holly—had so little.

The spruce was up near the center of the room. Boughs held strings of popcorn, colorful glass ornaments and bright red ribbons. The tree was lovely, but it was the memories of decorating it that made her spirit smile. The boys had made it fun. They had thrown popcorn at each other, and Eli had climbed the stepladder to set her mother's glass angel on the top of the tree.

Memories of previous years flashed across her mind, ones of laughter and good times, from that first, uncertain Christmas after the boys had arrived to just last year when both boys had picked her up and carried her around the house like the tree. Her "You put me down this minute" had been drowned out by their laughter.

She breathed in the tree's evergreen scent as she bent over her work, finishing a buttonhole. Good memories warmed her, but the sad ones held on to her like shadows. Her needle flashed in the light as she worked. She had to keep from thinking of Rafe and she would be all right. But the day's memories haunted her. The girl's delight as she glided on the swing in the snowfall. Rafe holding her hands in his. His gentleness as he brought up what he thought would be a terrible memory for her.

There is a small blessing in all this. I'm glad nothing bad happened to you, Cora. She remembered how his rich voice had dipped with concern, how his rugged features had melted with tenderness. No man had ever been so considerate of her feelings. It was as if he truly cared about her.

Her threaded needle stilled, as she remembered. He had been achingly kind to her. The love within her renewed, building stronger and bigger and taking deeper root. He probably had no idea at all that she had fallen for him. What would he think if he did? Would he run from town as fast as he could go? Or simply have compassion for the lonely spinster and her impossible hopes?

Fine, theirs was a love that was not meant to be. She could accept it. But she would always remember the man who walked into her life and changed it. She would always be grateful to him beyond measure.

She looked down at her work, realizing that she had forgotten to knot off the final buttonhole. She hid the thread, snipped if off and tried the button. A perfect fit.

When she shook the dress out to give it a critical look, she smiled. The sleeves were puffed, the collar was lace and the hem ruffled. She had reached a decision.

Chapter Nine

Rafe heard the light step hesitate outside his door. It sounded as if someone was being careful, didn't want to be heard. Odd, for it was early in the morning. Since trouble tended to find him now and again, he unsnapped his right holster just in case he needed to draw. When the knock came softly accompanied by the faint rustling of skirts, he should have felt relieved. There was no explaining the tight knot of warning in his gut, because it wasn't trouble. It was Cora Sims outside his door. No one else would knock so timidly.

He opened the door quietly, since Holly was still asleep in the next room. Cora was hardly more than a shadow in the dark hallway, bundled against the inclement weather and frosted with white. Snow was falling. That wasn't good for travel. No doubt the mountain passes would be rough going. He was concerned about Holly in the cold all day.

"I know it's early, and I'm sorry to bother you."

Cora's expressive eyes were all he could see behind the big hood she wore and the muffler wrapped around half her face. "I'm relieved to see you're up."

"I'm an early riser. Come in and get warm. I've got the stove going." He held the door for her, wondering what had brought her here. It wasn't appropriate for her to be here, not if she wanted to keep her pristine reputation. "You're not having any trouble with that lowlife Krantz? Did he get bail?"

"No. It's nothing like that." She was pale, maybe from the cold, maybe from a tough night. Heaven knew it had been tough here, as well. He glanced in on Holly, motionless beneath the quilts, and closed the door between the rooms tight. Best to let her sleep while she could.

"I finished one of Holly's dresses," Cora said. "I wanted to bring it over in case you two were…" She paused, looking uncertain, and unwound her scarf. Bits of ice tinkled to the floor and hissed when they hit the stove. She gestured toward the half-filled saddlebag. "You *are* packing. You're leaving town."

"I hope to head out this morning." He kept his heart closed and his voice hard. No sense in doing otherwise. It wasn't as if Cora Sims had come to declare her feelings for him. "It was good of you to think of Holly. Those other dresses I ordered. Let me pay you for those."

"No need." She held up her hand when he grabbed his billfold. "I didn't come here to be paid."

Of course not. She was too fine a lady for that. He took out a couple of bills, anyway, and dropped them on the dresser. "Holly will like the dress."

"It's made of fine-quality wool and will keep her toasty warm in cold weather like today." She pulled a wrapped bundle from her deep cloak pocket. She sure was a sight with snow melting in her hair like diamonds. The icy wind had put roses in her cheeks. She was even lovelier to him this morning, wind-tousled and dear. She had yet to look him in the eye. She was fussing with the length of flannel she had wrapped around the dress.

There was no mistaking the cool wall she had put between them. He felt awkward. "Maybe I left too quick yesterday. I don't remember if I thanked you for your hospitality."

"It was my pleasure." She shook the dress out and gave it a once-over. "I wanted Holly to have this to wear today."

"That's mighty considerate of you, Cora. I know she will like that. She's partial to that shade of purple."

"She told me." She had never felt more awkward in her life, standing in front of the man with his guns and his gruffness and hearing kindness warm his voice. She finally had Rafe Jones, fearsome bounty hunter, puzzled out. He might look dangerous on the outside, but he had a loving, generous heart, he who had never had a family or a home to call his own. Love bloomed ever new and she had to hide it. "When you left Holly with me in my shop that day, she was the best-behaved child I had seen in weeks."

"She hasn't given me a lick of trouble. She's a lot like you, Cora. Kind and gentle. I guess that's why it was easy to believe what I did."

"I would have liked nothing more than for it to be true."

"Me, too."

He sounded as desolate as she felt. She quaked deep inside, from being so near Rafe again or from what she had come to say, she didn't know. She held her hands out to the stove, letting the heat wash over her. It did not chase away the chill.

Seeing his hurt affected her more than she was prepared for. He was everything she had ever wanted. He was like a dream come true. But a romance between them would never be, so why was she hoping for one?

Foolish, that was all. She steeled her spine, gathering courage. She had something to tell him. After he heard it, she was certain he would finish packing, sling those saddlebags over his shoulder and stride out of her life. She would never see him again. Why would she? Their paths had never crossed before.

"I'm concerned about Holly." She hitched up her chin and her resolve.

"That's good of you, Cora. I know you care. That's just the way you are. I shouldn't have walked out on you yesterday. I was upset. I should have stayed and explained. None of this is your fault. I don't want you worrying about Holly. I'll make sure she's fine."

"Have you decided what to do?"

"Figured on taking her south with me. No sense staying in this hard climate if I don't have good reason to. I don't know what I'll do, but she isn't going back to that Beams woman. She's not going to an orphanage. I'm not sure what that leaves, but I'll find something."

"Let her stay with me."

"What?" He shook his head, not sure he had heard her right. "You'll keep her until I find a home for her?"

"No. I'll simply keep her, if she's willing. I raised two boys who weren't my own. Although Holly isn't related to me, I don't see what difference that will make."

"Are you sure? That's a lot to take on. Then, I suppose you know that."

"I've always wanted a little girl and at my age, I don't see any suitors offering to marry me. I think Holly and I could make each other happy." Her wide eyes were luminous with an emotion that put him to shame.

"You would do that?" He sank onto the edge of the mattress. His bones had turned to water. "You would take her in, just like that?"

"I'm fond of her. She has no home and no one to love her. I have a home and love to spare."

He rubbed his hands over his face. "I can't believe this. I hope you don't feel obligated because I thought you were her ma."

"No. It was a compliment." She wrapped her arms around her middle, as if comforting herself. She looked so vulnerable suddenly, and so delicate he had to fight feelings he didn't understand.

She amazed him, simple as that. "Not many women would want to raise someone else's child."

"Well, do you want to keep her?"

"It's not practical." Just like it wasn't practical to admit he cared more than he should. Funny, a month ago he never figured he was even capable of worthy feelings. Now he was stuffed full of them, and every one of them hurt like a bee sting. Because of her.

Everything within him ached with the need for her smile and her goodness in his life. She made him weak at the knees, and how he was going to find the gumption to ride out of town and away from her today, he didn't know. It was all he could do not to pull her to his chest and keep her warm and safe. It took all his might to hold back his feelings, but it was like lassoing the wind. He couldn't do it. Love blew through him like a chinook, thawing all the frozen places.

I love her. It was an all-out, no-conditions kind of love. He tried to tell himself he was a hundred times a fool, but it didn't do a lick of good. The emotion took root like a mountain, refusing to budge.

"I suppose she's still sleeping?" Cora glanced toward the closed door. Easy to read her affection for the child.

Yep, it was a good match. Maybe meant to be. The knot in his gut eased up. The broken pieces fell into place. The worry and burden left. He felt lighter than he ever had.

He turned his back on the half-packed bags. "Holly had a rough night. She took things real hard. I suppose you need to head over and open up your shop."

"Yes, business awaits."

"How about I bring her to you? You can tell her the good news yourself."

"I would like that very much." She neither smiled nor met his gaze. "I'd best be going."

"If you stay much longer, folks are going to talk."

"Let them. Any rumors going around town about me are a lot more exciting than I could ever dream of being. When my nephews came to live with me, folks thought they were my out-of-wedlock children I had refused to acknowledge." She avoided looking at Rafe as she crossed the small room, bypassing the money on the edge of the bureau, and reached for the door.

He brushed past her, moving fast for such a big man, and opened it. "I suppose some will say the same about Holly."

"Rumors tend to die down, especially when they're never true to begin with."

The hallway was a welcome escape. Once she was standing in those cloying shadows, she could relax a smidgeon. At least if a stray emotion crossed her face, he might not notice. Bittersweet, this love she had for him, at once lifting her with joy and weighing her down with regret.

"Good morning," she said quietly, daring to meet his gaze. "I shall see you and Holly later."

He nodded once in acknowledgment, nothing more, and stood granite still. All in black, he blended with the shadows almost completely. It was torture to think of what might have been. They were kindred souls, more alike than different. If only he could have fallen in love with her, she thought, forcing her feet to carry her down the hall toward the stairs. If only. He really could have been the one.

"Holly?" He rapped on her door. "You up? I hear you moving around in there."

"Yes, sir." Her voice was croaky. No doubt from all that sobbing most of the night through. The door opened to show a small girl with sorrow on her face.

Her hair was mussed, still in the braids from yester-day. The tear streaks had been scrubbed from her face. Her gaze went straight past him to the saddlebags loaded up and ready on top of the dresser. She sighed heavily, as if resigned to her fate. "I got all my things. S'pose we best get goin'."

Some might think she was strange, wanting to head back to a place where she had been poorly treated. He knew it was simply practical to face straight on what couldn't be changed. His chest cinched tight with prickly, expanding paternal feelings.

"You might want to change into the new dress Cora finished for you. She dropped it by this morning. She said she didn't want you to get chilled in this weather." He was determined not to tell her the rest, let Cora have the pleasure of breaking the good news. But Holly's pooling tears made him reassess things. He knelt down so he could look her in the eye. "There now. There's no sense to crying."

"I know. I can't s-stop." She reached into her skirt pocket and pulled out something shiny. Three copper pennies lay on her palm, catching the lamplight. "This is for you, Mr. Rafe."

"Aw, Holly, I can't take your money. I didn't find your ma. If I can't find her, she's nowhere to be found. I'm sorry."

"I know." Holly sniffed and dropped the money on the dresser by his saddlebags. "But it cost a lot to feed me and stuff. And the dress." She flattened her palm against the wrinkled green wool she wore. "Do I gotta give it back?"

"No, it's best you keep it." Hurt was steaming off her like heat from the stove, poor thing. He knew exactly how it was to hurt like that. "You best figure out a way to stop those tears, too, because someone here in town offered to let you live with them."

"Instead of Mrs. Beams? Really?" She drew up, hope chasing away her sorrow. "I'm a real good sweeper. I wash dishes up real good so there's not a single spot left on 'em. If I stay here in town, do you suppose I could see Miss Cora now and then? If I'm real good?"

"I reckon that could be arranged." He was itching to tell her the truth, but he was a man of his word. He wouldn't break a promise to Cora for anything. "Does this sound fine by you?"

"Yeah!" Holly flung her arms around his neck. "Thank you, Mr. Rafe. Thank you *so* much!"

Hard not to be affected by that. He patted her on the back awkwardly—he had never been hugged before— then peeled her off him. It was wonderful to see her happy. "You're welcome, little one. This will be a good place for you."

"As long as this missus is nicer than Mrs. Beams, I don't mind."

The girl thought she would still be working for her keep. He didn't know how to fix that without tipping his hand. "Trust me, this is much better than where you were."

"Yes, sir." She stared at the dresser top, full of his things. "I guess this means you're leavin'."

"Right after I drop you off. That means you had best

change into that new warm dress while I bundle up your things so I can get going. I have a long ride ahead of me." He stood and handed her the folded lilac-colored dress.

Her eyes lit up when she saw the frilly collar and dainty ruffles at the wrists and hem. Then the tears were back, and he rubbed a hand over the top of her head. He knew what it was like to be overwhelmed with too much feeling. When you were used to a tough, lonely road in life, kindness was a rare and great mercy.

"You go in your room and change." He turned his back so she couldn't see how hard this was for him. He wasn't used to attachments; he wasn't used to having to let them go, either. The snow beat at the window with a vengeance, and he was glad of it. Nothing like riding in a vicious, freezing storm to make a man forget his troubles.

Not that he was ever going to completely forget, he thought as he scooped up Holly's pennies and dropped them into one of his extra packs for her things. It was still snowing outside, coming down like heartache. He could just make out a woman with a brown hood and coat stepping out onto the street.

Cora. His soul brimmed with sadness, remembering how beautiful she had been in the lamplight. Her gentle kindness had done more than capture his heart. It had changed him. Unless he figured out a way to reach out to her and soon, he'd spend the rest of his days trying not to remember the woman he had left behind.

Chapter Ten

It was snow hitting her lashes and nothing else, Cora told herself firmly as she crossed the street in front of Rafe's hotel. She had enough on her mind with having Holly come live with her. She did not need to dwell on what had never been hers to begin with. Rafe Jones might have claimed her heart, but she had not claimed his.

The wind gusted, howling against the building's eaves and whipping down the street. Snow scudded in pristine clouds and tangled with her skirt ruffles. She stumbled the last few paces across the empty street and gladly took refuge in a small alcove. She brushed the snow off her face and the front of her coat. Then the hair on the back of her neck bristled, as a shadow detached itself from the dark corner of the tailor's shop.

Panic spilled into her veins. She recognized the shape of the broad-brimmed hat and the curve of an unshaven jaw. A cigarette flicked onto the boards at her feet, and before she could take a single step, his hand hooked around her shoulder, dangerously close to her throat.

"You don't listen so good, lady." Krantz's voice was as gritty as his face. He was unwashed and reeked of alcohol. "I told you not to talk to the sheriff, so you had that bounty hunter do it. Well, word is he's leavin' town and now you're in real trouble. I'm not goin' to jail over a skirt like you."

She gulped, panic turning to terror. She wanted to run, but his fingers were biting into the dip between her neck and her shoulder, holding her captive. His eyes were empty and cold as he thumbed back the hammer of his revolver. When the cold metal pressed into her temple, she bit her bottom lip, refusing to whimper.

"Here's what you're gonna do." His fingers tightened without mercy, forcing her to her knees.

Streaks of pain shot down her arm and up her neck, and she blinked hard against it, trying to make sense of what he was saying.

"You're gonna go to the sheriff and tell him you were mistaken. You get those charges dropped. If you don't, I'll— What the—?" The gun whipped away from her temple and flew out of his hand.

She watched in amazement as Rafe grabbed the man by the throat and lifted him off his feet. She had never seen such a thing. He radiated strength and controlled fury. He was invincible as he tossed Krantz on the ground and put a gun to his head.

Thank God for Rafe, she thought. Thank the Lord Rafe was unharmed and she was, too.

"Are you all right, Cora?" he bit out, breathing hard as he handcuffed his quarry to a hitching post.

"Y-yes." Her hands shook so badly, she couldn't press them to her face to hide her fear or her awe of the man. Her careful control was shattered. Relief shivered through her with enough force to make her teeth clack together. She sat down completely on the cold boards. Maybe if she propped her elbows on her knees, she would be able to hide her face from him.

"Cora?" He came closer, his stride fierce enough to vibrate the boards. He towered over her, sheltering her from the sting of the gusting wind. "Are you hurt?"

Tenderness laced his words. His tenderness touched her deeply, and she had no strength, no defenses. They lay in pieces like the snow falling to the boardwalk in front of her. She took her hands from her face, wholly vulnerable to him, her deepest self revealed. "No, Rafe. I'm not hurt."

"I thought for a moment there…" He helped her to her feet, agony stark on his chiseled face. "I saw the gun to your head and I didn't know if I could get to you in time. If he had pulled the trigger…"

"He didn't." Her terror faded completely when she saw his. "I'm all right, Rafe. You stopped him. I think he was t-trying to scare me."

"I see. He wanted the charges dropped." He cradled her face with his hands.

She could feel his fear fading. Love warmed the storm gray of his eyes. His hands against her face were a tender comfort she could not deny. He cared for her. No, he more than cared for her. Everything within her ached for him. She needed this man the way the snow needed the earth, the way the sun needed the sky.

"I can't get that image out of my head." He rubbed at her temple, where the gun had been. "It nearly killed me. All I could think about was, what if I lost you. What if—"

She never knew what he meant to say next. His mouth slanted over hers, hovering a moment before claiming her. His kiss was pure sweetness, better than the most poignant poem and more poignant than the most moving hymn. Her soul sighed, her world hushed. A sense of rightness wrapped around her like hope. He was kissing her. Rafe Jones had chosen to kiss her. Thankfulness left her breathless as he broke away.

"Think of the rumors that are going to start up now." She smiled. She was sure, absolutely sure. This was the man she would love for the rest of her life.

"Those rumors might get even worse after I move in with you and Holly." His slow smile was paradise.

"Oh, you plan on moving in with me?"

"After the wedding." His jaw tightened. Anxiety rolled off him. "That is, if you will have me."

"Rafe, I—"

"Wait." He cut her off before she could answer. She had to be sure. He couldn't take it if she said yes to him on the power of emotion and changed her mind once she had a chance to think about it. He wanted to give her that chance now.

He took a step away and nodded toward Krantz. "Now you've seen what I am. What I do. I make my living with my gun. It might not always be that way, but it is right now."

"Rafe, I know that. It's you, the man you are, who matters to me." Her fingers curled into his coat, holding on to him, holding on and not letting go. "You matter to me very much."

That meant the world to him. Devotion to her filled his chest, nearly lifting him off the ground. "Enough to let me come courting?"

"I thought you said you wanted to marry me." So vulnerable, with her heart showing.

He figured his was, too, and there was nothing wrong with that. He gently brushed stray curls from her face. "Sure I want to marry you, but a man ought to come courting first, don't you reckon?"

"I do, but please keep in mind I would like a September wedding." She gazed up at him with tears silvering her eyes, making her look more beautiful than ever. She made him feel ten feet tall, as if he belonged. As if he was loved.

"September sounds awful fine to me." He kissed her again. Powerful tenderness moved through him like a hymn. Immeasurable caring serenaded his soul. When he broke the kiss, he didn't move away. He liked being close to her, liked being the man who would love her, cherish her and protect her for the rest of his life. "I love you, Cora."

"I love you, Rafe." She meant it.

Even a skeptic like him could see it. "You're the first ever to say that to me."

"Believe me, it won't be the last time you hear it." She wrapped her arms around him.

He held her tight, sheltering her from the brunt of the wind, letting the rare gift of her love change him into a man who believed in happy endings. He held her, letting the snow envelop them, breathing in the security of her affection and cherishing the wisps of her hair like silk against his jaw, the warm puff of her breath on his neck and the way her cheek lay against the top of his chest.

His one and only prayer had come true. How about that? He pondered that a moment, feeling the wind at his back. As if heaven knew what he was thinking, the snowfall eased up, and down the street the church steeple appeared like a gentle reminder through the haze of snow. God hadn't forgotten even a man like him. He wasn't alone. Humbled, he drew Cora closer, doubly grateful for the blessing of her love.

"Are you sure we're goin' the right way?" Holly wrapped her arms around her middle, as if for comfort. Her face was peaked with worry, although he had tried to reassure her.

"I told you to trust me, didn't I?"

"Yeah." She didn't sound too sure as they crossed the street.

"Morning, Reverend." He nodded to the man of the cloth standing in the falling snow on the street corner. He dropped a few dollar coins into the collection pot.

"Good morning, Mr. Jones." Hadly winked. "I expect I'll be seeing you in church come Sunday?"

"I expect you will." Rafe laid a hand on Holly's shoulder to nudge her along the boardwalk past the land office and the shoemaker's. "Don't you worry. It's not far now."

"Miss Cora's shop is right there. Can we stop in to see her first? Before we get to my new home?"

"Look at that. Cora's spotted us through the window. Looks to me like she's been keeping watch for us." His soul filled with joy as Cora stepped out her door, a fancy blue shawl draped around her shoulders. Love radiated from her, making her unbearably beautiful. "You go on over to Cora. She's got something to tell you."

"Does she know who I'm goin' to live with?"

He didn't have to answer. Cora did it for him. She held out her hand. "Holly, I've been waiting for you. I need your help choosing things for your new room. Actually, you will have one of my nephew's old rooms, but we will make it pretty for you."

"For me? You mean I'm gonna work for you?" Holly hiccuped, caught between a gasp of surprise and a sob. "I'm a good sweeper. I can get every bit of dirt."

Holly stumbled forward, talking at once and so fast she didn't let the need for air or the tears rolling down her cheeks stop her. "I'll sweep extra hard for you, Miss Cora. I can keep every bit of snow off your boardwalk. I'm extra good at windows. And I can learn to sew, I know I can, and help you so you will let me stay on."

The child thought she wanted her to work? Undone, she pulled the girl close and held her tight. "No, Holly, you don't understand. I don't want you to work for me. I want you to live with me. To be my daughter, my own little girl. Wait, that's not right. Rafe and I want you to be *our* little girl."

"But nobody wants me like that."

"We do." She looked at Rafe and he nodded. They didn't need words, because his heart was her own.

As snow sifted over her like pieces of perfection, she knew God had been leading her here to Rafe and to Holly all along. She had her very own hero, a wedding to sew for and a happy life ahead filled with true and everlasting love. She remembered to send a prayer heavenward. *Thank you, Lord.* She held out her hand, bringing Rafe closer. They were together, a family, and just in time for Christmas.

Epilogue

Christmas Eve, two years later

"Merry Christmas, Mrs. Jones," Rhett Jorgenson called out from a few storefronts down, where he was sweeping his stretch of boardwalk. "Closing up early today?"

"Yes, thank the Lord. Merry Christmas to you, too." She nodded to him as she locked the door. The manager she had hired to run the shop was a blessing. She didn't need to worry about the bank deposit, which was good since Joshua looked as if he was waking up from his nap. Infinite love blazed through her as she watched her son. Tucked warmly in his carriage, he yawned hugely. His eyes fluttered open, he stretched and slipped back into sleep.

What a relief. For a three-month-old, he sure had a set of lungs. He could drown out the tolling of the church bells.

"Merry Christmas, Mrs. Jones." A rich baritone rumbled behind her.

She warmed like melted butter at her husband's voice. Rafe. He took her breath away, as he did every time she saw him. His black Stetson shaded his chiseled features, and with his brawny shoulders set and his powerful gait, he looked as if he could move mountains with a single push. The waning sunshine seemed to find him, and he walked in the light.

"Merry Christmas, Mr. Jones." As always, great joy sparkled through her simply from being with him. She felt like those clouds sailing through the sky, light and swift and boundless. "Have you closed up your shop for the day?"

"Sure did. Gunsmithing isn't in demand on Christmas Eve." He reached her side and hauled her into his arms, not caring that they were in plain sight. His kiss was perfection. "I missed you, Cora. I don't feel right if I'm not with you."

"Neither do I." That was what real love did. It made the world right. She needed him more than air and sunlight. She was not complete without him. Just as he was not complete without her.

Love softened his face as he settled his arm on her shoulders. They strolled down the boardwalk together, pushing their precious son in his carriage.

The jangle of a hand bell rose above the sounds of the busy town. Reverend Hadly's son, Austin, stood on the street corner with a collection tin on a stand in front of him. "Merry Christmas, Mr. and Mrs. Jones. You wouldn't be able to spare a few pennies for the orphan fund, would you?"

"You already know the answer to that." She opened her reticule and extricated a coin. She dropped the five-dollar gold piece into the tin. Before the new minister could comment, she explained, "God has been very good to us. We may as well share some of our blessings with others."

"Thank you kindly." Austin smiled broadly. "I'll see you in church tonight."

They walked along, talking of their plans for the evening and of the gifts they had hidden away for Holly and Joshua. They said hello to acquaintances and stopped to exchange pleasantries with friends. Emmett drove by with his team and loaded sleigh, looking busy with his last delivery for the day. He tipped his hat, promising to be by for Christmas Eve supper when he was done.

"Cora! Rafe!" Holly waltzed down the church steps in her best dress of blue velvet. She had grown tall and stately, but she was still their little girl. She buttoned her coat as she dashed toward them. "Choir practice went perfectly. I can't wait for tonight. You can hear my solo."

"I'm looking forward to hearing you sing." Cora held out her free hand, welcoming the girl. "You have a lovely voice, Holly."

"Thank you. Let me take Joshua." Holly, a proud big sister, eagerly took charge of the carriage.

Yes, life was sheer bliss. What a difference two years had made, Cora thought. She had gone from being a lonely spinster to being a happy wife and mother because of God's grace and Rafe's love.

"What's that look on your face?" He leaned close, his voice low. "I don't know it."

"I'm thinking of you." She stopped in the lane, where trees arched overhead from either side. She could hear the merry sounds of town behind her, the toll of the church bell and the hush that came before snowfall. The world—her world—was incredibly beautiful.

Gazing into his loving eyes, it was easy to see their future, each day passing more treasured than the next and each year a precious gift. There would be another baby one day. Birthdays and occasions to celebrate. And most of all, there would be this man at her side, bound to her heart, a part of her soul. The man she would love for eternity.

"I would be lost if you had not come into my life, Rafe. You have given me everything."

"That's how I feel about you." Endless love shone in his eyes. "I would have been forever lost, Cora, but you found me. You are my happy ending."

The snow chose that moment to fall. The hush became singing. The blessed day felt transformed. Snow danced over them like grace from heaven, God's amazing grace. Bound by love, Rafe took his wife's hand and they walked home together.

* * * * *

DISCUSSION QUESTIONS

1 Rafe agrees to help Holly find her mother. What does this say about his character? Why do you think he decides to help her? How do we know he's a good guy?

2. When Cora sees rough-looking Rafe on the street, how does she treat him? What does this say about her character? When we first meet Cora, she is officially a spinster, feeling past her prime. How does Rafe change that? How does he touch her heart?

3. What do you think Cora, Rafe and Holly have learned about the power of hope? Of kindness? Of grace?

4. At the beginning of the story, Rafe cannot imagine living a life like the others, with family and friends and a place to belong. By the end of the book, he finds that life with Cora and Holly. How did this happen? What changed him? What has he learned?

5. Cora believes in the power of kindness. How does this affect her own life? What effect does it have on Rafe? On Holly?

6. What values of Christmas do you find in this story? What do those values mean to you?

REQUEST YOUR FREE BOOKS!

2 FREE INSPIRATIONAL NOVELS
PLUS 2
FREE
MYSTERY GIFTS

Love Inspired

YES! Please send me 2 FREE Love Inspired® novels and my 2 FREE mystery gifts (gifts are worth about $10). After receiving them, if I don't wish to receive any more books, I can return the shipping statement marked "cancel." If I don't cancel, I will receive 6 brand-new novels every month and be billed just $4.74 per book in the U.S. or $5.24 per book in Canada. That's a savings of at least 21% off the cover price. It's quite a bargain! Shipping and handling is just 50¢ per book in the U.S. and 75¢ per book in Canada.* I understand that accepting the 2 free books and gifts places me under no obligation to buy anything. I can always return a shipment and cancel at any time. Even if I never buy another book, the two free books and gifts are mine to keep forever.

105/305 IDN F49N

Name _____ (PLEASE PRINT) _____

Address _____ Apt. # _____

City _____ State/Prov. _____ Zip/Postal Code _____

Signature (if under 18, a parent or guardian must sign)

Mail to the **Harlequin® Reader Service:**
IN U.S.A.: P.O. Box 1867, Buffalo, NY 14240-1867
IN CANADA: P.O. Box 609, Fort Erie, Ontario L2A 5X3

**Are you a subscriber to Love Inspired books
and want to receive the larger-print edition?
Call 1-800-873-8635 or visit www.ReaderService.com.**

* Terms and prices subject to change without notice. Prices do not include applicable taxes. Sales tax applicable in N.Y. Canadian residents will be charged applicable taxes. Offer not valid in Quebec. This offer is limited to one order per household. Not valid for current subscribers to Love Inspired books. All orders subject to credit approval. Credit or debit balances in a customer's account(s) may be offset by any other outstanding balance owed by or to the customer. Please allow 4 to 6 weeks for delivery. Offer available while quantities last.

Your Privacy—The Harlequin® Reader Service is committed to protecting your privacy. Our Privacy Policy is available online at www.ReaderService.com or upon request from the Harlequin Reader Service.
We make a portion of our mailing list available to reputable third parties that offer products we believe may interest you. If you prefer that we not exchange your name with third parties, or if you wish to clarify or modify your communication preferences, please visit us at www.ReaderService.com/consumerschoice or write to us at Harlequin Reader Service Preference Service, P.O. Box 9062, Buffalo, NY 14269. Include your complete name and address.

LIDIR13R

REQUEST YOUR FREE BOOKS!
2 FREE RIVETING INSPIRATIONAL NOVELS
PLUS 2 FREE MYSTERY GIFTS

YES! Please send me 2 FREE Love Inspired® Suspense novels and my 2 FREE mystery gifts (gifts are worth about $10). After receiving them, if I don't wish to receive any more books, I can return the shipping statement marked "cancel." If I don't cancel, I will receive 4 brand-new novels every month and be billed just $4.74 per book in the U.S. or $5.24 per book in Canada. That's a savings of at least 21% off the cover price. It's quite a bargain! Shipping and handling is just 50¢ per book in the U.S. and 75¢ per book in Canada.* I understand that accepting the 2 free books and gifts places me under no obligation to buy anything. I can always return a shipment and cancel at any time. Even if I never buy another book, the two free books and gifts are mine to keep forever.

123/323 IDN F5AN

Name	(PLEASE PRINT)	
Address		Apt. #
City	State/Prov.	Zip/Postal Code

Signature (if under 18, a parent or guardian must sign)

Mail to the **Harlequin® Reader Service:**
IN U.S.A.: P.O. Box 1867, Buffalo, NY 14240-1867
IN CANADA: P.O. Box 609, Fort Erie, Ontario L2A 5X3

**Are you a current subscriber to Love Inspired Suspense books
and want to receive the larger-print edition?
Call 1-800-873-8635 or visit www.ReaderService.com.**

* Terms and prices subject to change without notice. Prices do not include applicable taxes. Sales tax applicable in N.Y. Canadian residents will be charged applicable taxes. Offer not valid in Quebec. This offer is limited to one order per household. Not valid for current subscribers to Love Inspired Suspense books. All orders subject to credit approval. Credit or debit balances in a customer's account(s) may be offset by any other outstanding balance owed by or to the customer. Please allow 4 to 6 weeks for delivery. Offer available while quantities last.

LISDIR13R

REQUEST YOUR FREE BOOKS!

2 FREE INSPIRATIONAL NOVELS
PLUS 2
FREE
MYSTERY GIFTS

Love Inspired
HISTORICAL
INSPIRATIONAL HISTORICAL ROMANCE

YES! Please send me 2 FREE Love Inspired® Historical novels and my 2 FREE mystery gifts (gifts are worth about $10). After receiving them, if I don't wish to receive any more books, I can return the shipping statement marked "cancel." If I don't cancel, I will receive 4 brand-new novels every month and be billed just $4.74 per book in the U.S. or $5.24 per book in Canada. That's a savings of at least 21% off the cover price. It's quite a bargain! Shipping and handling is just 50¢ per book in the U.S. and 75¢ per book in Canada.* I understand that accepting the 2 free books and gifts places me under no obligation to buy anything. I can always return a shipment and cancel at any time. Even if I never buy another book, the two free books and gifts are mine to keep forever.

102/302 IDN F5CY

Name _____ (PLEASE PRINT) _____

Address _____ Apt. # _____

City _____ State/Prov. _____ Zip/Postal Code _____

Signature (if under 18, a parent or guardian must sign)

Mail to the Harlequin® Reader Service:
IN U.S.A.: P.O. Box 1867, Buffalo, NY 14240-1867
IN CANADA: P.O. Box 609, Fort Erie, Ontario L2A 5X3

Want to try two free books from another series?
Call 1-800-873-8635 or visit www.ReaderService.com.

* Terms and prices subject to change without notice. Prices do not include applicable taxes. Sales tax applicable in N.Y. Canadian residents will be charged applicable taxes. Offer not valid in Quebec. This offer is limited to one order per household. Not valid for current subscribers to Love Inspired Historical books. All orders subject to credit approval. Credit or debit balances in a customer's account(s) may be offset by any other outstanding balance owed by or to the customer. Please allow 4 to 6 weeks for delivery. Offer available while quantities last.

Your Privacy—The Harlequin® Reader Service is committed to protecting your privacy. Our Privacy Policy is available online at www.ReaderService.com or upon request from the Harlequin Reader Service.

We make a portion of our mailing list available to reputable third parties that offer products we believe may interest you. If you prefer that we not exchange your name with third parties, or if you wish to clarify or modify your communication preferences, please visit us at www.ReaderService.com/consumerschoice or write to us at Harlequin Reader Service Preference Service, P.O. Box 9062, Buffalo, NY 14269. Include your complete name and address.

LIHDIR13R

REQUEST YOUR FREE BOOKS!

2 FREE CHRISTIAN NOVELS
PLUS 2
FREE
MYSTERY GIFTS

HEARTSONG
PRESENTS

YES! Please send me 2 Free Heartsong Presents novels and my 2 FREE mystery gifts (gifts are worth about $10). After receiving them, if I don't wish to receive any more books I can return the shipping statement marked "cancel." If I don't cancel, I will receive 4 brand-new novels every month and be billed just $4.24 per book in the U.S. and $5.24 per book in Canada. That's a savings of at least 20% off the cover price. It's quite a bargain! Shipping and handling is just 50¢ per book in the U.S. and 75¢ per book in Canada.* I understand that accepting the 2 free books and gifts places me under no obligation to buy anything. I can always return a shipment and cancel at any time. Even if I never buy another book, the two free books and gifts are mine to keep forever.

159/359 HDN FVYK

Name	(PLEASE PRINT)	
Address		Apt. #
City	State	Zip

Signature (if under 18, a parent or guardian must sign)

Mail to the **Harlequin®** Reader Service:
IN U.S.A.: P.O. Box 1867, Buffalo, NY 14240-1867

* Terms and prices subject to change without notice. Prices do not include applicable taxes. Sales tax applicable in N.Y. This offer is limited to one order per household. Not valid for current subscribers to Heartsong Presents books. All orders subject to credit approval. Credit or debit balances in a customer's account(s) may be offset by any other outstanding balance owed by or to the customer. Please allow 4 to 6 weeks for delivery. Offer available while quantities last. Offer valid only in the U.S.

Your Privacy—The Harlequin® Reader Service is committed to protecting your privacy. Our Privacy Policy is available online at www.ReaderService.com or upon request from the Harlequin Reader Service.
We make a portion of our mailing list available to reputable third parties that offer products we believe may interest you. If you prefer that we not exchange your name with third parties, or if you wish to clarify or modify your communication preferences, please visit us at www.ReaderService.com/consumerschoice or write to us at Harlequin Reader Service Preference Service, P.O. Box 9062, Buffalo, NY 14269. Include your complete name and address.

Reader Service.com

Manage your account online!
- Review your order history
- Manage your payments
- Update your address

> *We've designed
> the Harlequin® Reader Service
> website just for you.*

Enjoy all the features!
- Reader excerpts from any series
- Respond to mailings and special monthly offers
- Discover new series available to you
- Browse the Bonus Bucks catalog
- Share your feedback

Visit us at:

ReaderService.com